BEETLECREEK
William Demby

Afterword by Herbert Hill

 BARD BOOKS/PUBLISHED BY AVON

AVON BOOKS
A division of
The Hearst Corporation
959 Eighth Avenue
New York, New York 10019
Copyright 1950 by William Demby.
Published by arrangement with the author.

Afterword Copyright © 1967 by Avon Book Division,
The Hearst Corporation.

First Printing (Avon Library Edition) January, 1967
Second Printing (Bard Edition) October, 1969

Printed in the U.S.A.

PART ONE

■ CHAPTER ONE

Always when he looked in the mirror his eyes were different. Sometimes they peered from out of the broken glass asking an unanswerable question, sometimes they were angry and damning, sometimes they were sullen and brooding—too often they were the eyes of a dead man, jellied and blank. This ritual of looking at himself went on every day as soon as he got out of bed. His thick, blunt fingers would clutch at each other, moving back and forth slowly like the antennae of insects. His long, fleshy nose with its countless red pin pricks would expand and contract in time to his breathing and the gray-striped lips that refused to open over the severe outward slant of the front teeth would strain themselves into the subtlest kind of smile. There were deep vertical wrinkles along his cheek and at the corners of his eyes which gave an impression of kindliness. These wrinkles moved up and down, restlessly recording the changing climates of his emotions. Thus he would stand, sometimes for over an hour, a silent ugly man who could no longer tell whether he was inside the mirror or inside himself.

Bill Trapp had not long been at the mirror that afternoon when he heard a rustling in the bushes near the stonewall. Quickly he ran his hand through his matted hair and put on a huge felt hat. He walked very slowly, half on tiptoes, until he arrived at a bush. There, he kneeled down on the cold mud and parted the branches. He waited until he heard the rustling again and then rose high enough to see the intruders. His heart beat fast as it always did. Always when they came he would look into their faces. He would be filled with uncontrollable excitement knowing that he was seeing them while they couldn't see him. Faster and faster his heart would beat until, filled with shame and rage, he would rush out at them waving his arms wildly, shouting,

7

almost screaming long after they had disappeared down the road.

In fifteen years he had had only one visitor, a tramp who came to his door to beg because he was too proud to beg from the Negroes down by the bridge. He gave coffee and sandwiches to this tramp, who, as soon as he had finished eating, went away. Once some colored ladies started to come into the yard and he chased them away with his shotgun. Sometimes, out of a furious impulse to break the clammy silence, he would begin singing songs he had heard in the towns along the river. Once a week, when he went to town to fetch the provisions he needed to live on or to sell the fruits and vegetables he grew, he found himself still talking in whispers, and people who spoke with him then would whisper too.

This time there were four boy Negroes under the tree. Three of them, wild-eyed and grinning, were signaling frantically to the boy in the tree to hurry and throw down to them some of the waxy, red apples.

The face of the boy in the tree held Bill Trapp's attention. He had never seen this boy before although the faces of the others were all familiar. All the boys were between the ages of thirteen and fifteen but the face of this boy seemed at once younger and older. It was a gentle, pear-shaped face; the eyes were clever and slanted and there was a serious monkey expression on it as the boy tried to concentrate on reaching for the apples.

For almost ten minutes the white man watched. Soon he felt the familiar itchy nervousness coming. But instead of rage this time, he was filled with curiosity. Very careful not to rustle the leaves, he rose to his feet; then, slowly and silently, he walked toward where the boys were crouching.

As soon as they saw him, the boys on the ground fled shrieking, but he paid no attention to them. His eyes were on the boy in the tree and toward him he walked. Even as he came nearer and nearer the tree and saw that the boy made no move to escape, he felt that it was he himself who should be fleeing. Closer and closer he came to the tree and slower and slower became his footsteps. Then, as he realized there was no backing away, that he would have to speak to the boy, he was filled with complete panic. His sweaty fingers deep through the holes in his pocket pulled at the long hairs of his thigh.

The boy's eyes swept back and forth like the eyes of a movable valentine. His pouting lips were parted and he breathed with difficulty.

"Come down," Bill Trapp said, and while the words were still forming on his lips, he realized that by an act of his own will he was ending his fifteen years of silence and solitude.

He bade the boy Negro sit down on the porch while he went into the shack, mumbling incoherently that he had something to do. The moment he was inside, he peeped out the window and was surprised that the boy seemed not to be frightened but was relaxed against the two-by-four support of the roof. Realizing that the boy was not going to run away as he had at first hoped and feared, he experienced a strange feeling—a feeling of tenderness toward the boy and indeed, to all people. With no more preparation than that—in one instant—the fifteen-year-old desire to be alone was wiped away.

He ran to the mirror and looked at himself. He tried to smile. For years and years he hadn't washed his teeth. He found a broken piece of comb and tried to do something with his hair. He found two cracked cups and filled them with cider he had bought recently from the A & P. These he carried out to the boy on the porch who turned with wide-eyed surprise to face him. Still trembling, he offered one of the cups to the boy. They drank nervously and silently. Neither would look at the other.

"I didn' mean nothing by it," the boy said finally, holding the empty cup close to his ear as if he were listening to a seashell.

The sound of the boy's voice came as a shock to him, came as a clap of thunder, and he didn't know what he should say.

"You kids should ask for the fruit . . . all you had to do was ask and you coulda had all you wanted."

The cider was all gone—they each had had three cups—and there was no longer any excuse for the boy to stay. Once the boy turned toward him and looked straight into his eyes. Bill Trapp blushed and tried desperately to pry his mouth open in some kind of smile. He felt dizzy, tingling all

9

over with thoughts that appeared and disappeared in his consciousness like so many fireflies. He kept saying to himself: Chase the kid away, give him a bawling out and chase him away. Instead, he asked the boy his name. And then asked him where he lived, realizing after a few moments that he was having a conversation with him. The boy's name was Johnny Johnson. He was from Pittsburgh and had come to stay with his aunt and uncle while his mother was in the hospital. He wanted to look at the boy's face again to see if he was scared. He found himself rooting in his nostril, wiping his thick finger on his pants. But the boy didn't see this and he was relieved. He coughed and began to fidget.

"I could tell you something, Johnny, about being here all by yourself. I never would of chased nobody away 'cept they don't ask. I come from respectable folks and I respect people's property." But he saw that the boy wasn't listening.

When he looked toward where the boy was looking, he saw the gate burst open and a tall, distracted looking Negro run into the yard. He looked questioning at Johnny and even moved closer to the boy as if to protect himself.

"That's my uncle," Johnny said.

"What's he want?" Bill Trapp asked. "I've got my rights and I respect people's property. . . ."

"What're you doing with that boy?" the man demanded, grasping hold of Johnny's hand as if to pull him away.

Bill Trapp couldn't open his mouth to speak. He was deaf. There was too much sound about him. He could hear the clock on the table inside the house. What did it mean, having these people on his porch? He was afraid, but he had gone this far, there was no turning back.

"He wasn't hurting me, Uncle David," the boy said. "We was just talking."

"I respect people's property, Mister. I'm a law abidin citizen. I'm an old man now. But I don't hurt nobody. See all this place here. I built it up. We come from respectable folks." He got up and went into the house. When he came out he brought a bottle of dandelion wine. The Negro man and boy became very quiet.

They drank; their breaths and sighs were in unison. They stole looks at each other from out of the corner of their eyes. And then the Negro man laughed.

"So you're Mister Bill Trapp?" he said. "Well, sir, it's a pleasure to be here with you. A real pleasure."

"I don't have many visitors," Bill Trapp said. "I'm what you call a retired man. I've done my share. But I could tell you a thing or two about being here all alone, no one to talk to. Gets so you forget a lot of things. But we come from respectable folks. I don't mean nobody no harm."

The light faded to near darkness and the three of them were still sitting there. To Bill Trapp it was like something out of his fantastic dreams to have the Negro man and boy on his porch. There was a lot of talk. The Negro man talked continuously with a nervous, jerky flow of words that Bill Trapp finally gave up trying to follow. He had been too long alone. He remembered a warning feeling which came to him, a feeling which as soon as it came he hastened to brush away. He felt vaguely that he was in danger. But dominating all that he was feeling was the tremendous resolution not to go back to the lonely ways of before. He was conscious of a change of life in him, a change that seemed to have come suddenly but which he knew was prepared for years before.

Before his visitors left, he recklessly promised to meet the man that night, promised to go with him to Telrico's Café.

Alone once more, still trembling, he went to the mirror and looked at his eyes. They were milky damp. His eyelids were sweating. This time he stayed at the mirror until it was so dark he could see only the slightest reflection on the whites of his eyes. What kind of mad thing had he let himself in for? He stayed up just long enough to warm himself a can of beans. By six o'clock he was undressed and in bed speculating on whether or not he would get up to meet the Negro man. He was hot and sweating. He kept the lamp lit so that he could watch the clock. Slowly and meticulously, his clumsy fingers pulled hairs from his thighs.

CHAPTER TWO

JOHNNY JOHNSON, completely undressed except for his underwear, lay across the bed. A *Doctor Zorro and the Dope Smugglers* lay unopened across his stomach. He had wanted to go outside where he knew the boys were waiting to hear what happened at Bill Trapp's, but, because he had been caught, his Aunt Mary had been very strict with him. He could hear them whooping and laughing and every once in a while he could hear the Leader calling his dog.

He looked around at the pink-rosed wallpaper. Everything was strange here, he decided. From the time when his cousin put him on the bus and he'd been left alone, sitting all by himself in the back of the bus watching the smooth West Virginia mountains already tinted by patches of red and brown gold, he had had the feeling he sometimes had when walking on a strange street in a strange neighborhood, a feeling like walking up the aisle of a full movie house when the lights were on, seeing all the faces, yet not seeing—feeling. A feeling of vague, itchy fear.

And that afternoon sitting with the old white man on his porch at the May Farm, drinking cider and feeling the man's terrible eyes on him, seeing the shack and the funny shaped trees and the big flowers like nothing he had ever seen before, he had had the same feeling.

He wished he were back in his room at home in Pittsburgh. He rose and sat on the edge of the bed and turned on another light. He stared toward the closed door as if he expected the source of his fears to come in.

From downstairs, as he held his breath waiting, came the sound of his aunt's sobbing. Now with the fear was the conflicting desire to go to her, to put his arms around her waist as he remembered he used to do many years ago to his mother. He jumped up. His book fell to the floor and the sound startled him so that he couldn't close his mouth.

Quickly he slipped into his trousers and shoes and went

12

to the living room where she sat crumpled in the rocker.

"Aunt Mary," he began, and the sound of the words seemed to crystallize and echo and echo through the room, mixing finally with the hoarse sound of her crying. She became rigid and their eyes met. A look, first of shame and afterwards of anger, darted across her eyes in quick succession.

"Well, I'll be! What are you doing up and sneaking around the house for?" she snarled.

The savagery of her tone chilled him. He stuttered, "Can-n-n I . . . can I do something for you?"

"You can get right upstairs to your room, that's what you can do. We don't have to put up with any of that Pittsburgh smart-aleckness out of you!"

He ran up the stairs and slammed his door. He was ashamed now to have gone downstairs to his aunt. He fell across the bed and lay there shaking until he felt sleep coming—sleep and the dreaming.

He knew how it would be, even to the soft, billowy feeling of the bed being pushed upward from underneath. He faced toward the corner from which it would come, always the same:

First, the silverness that was like a cloud of mercury that formed from nothing. Then a hot, electric feeling as if the room had been filled with electricity. Then a feeling of movement as if everything in the room were vibrating from a streetcar running overhead. Then the rain which wasn't exactly like rain but rather a feeling of millions and trillions of things falling. And then, the procession:

That night there was his mother dressed in a white nightgown from the hospital that was stained green and brown with blood that dripped from her neck. She was smiling but was convulsed by silent coughing. Very slowly she walked toward him. He squinched his eyes so he wouldn't see her. Closer and closer she walked until she had passed over his stomach. When he looked up, there was blood dripping on him and he could see that she was still smiling and nodding her head and coughing.

Then there was the old white man, Bill Trapp. There was a flock of sheep with him and he had a staff like a Bible shepherd. And the sheep were all afraid and kept prancing up and down like nervous horses in a lightning storm—like

13

the horses did that time at the county fair when he went with his father. Bill Trapp would raise his hand and smile and the sheep would be even more frightened, prancing higher and higher. And when they came too close, he ducked his head so their hoofs wouldn't hurt him, but they passed over him so lightly, he didn't feel anything. Then the old man glided to him. His face was so close he could look right into his deep, strange eyes, and the eyes were green and there were long, green hairs growing out of the corners of them. It didn't look like Bill Trapp though. The face was sly and young, a combination of the Leader's face and the old man's, a shiny, hazy face that could be identified only by the hat. . . .

The dream would have gone on except that he was awakened by the creaking of the door. His sleep muscles tightened as he tried to hold onto the warmth and color of the dream.

He knew his Aunt Mary was there, a ghostlike figure in her nightgown—the odor of her bedclothing more than the sight of her indicating her presence.

"Johnny! Johnny! You 'wake?" She touched him lightly under the chin and her cool hand felt pleasant in the hot, sweaty groove at his neck.

He kept very still, holding his breath, waiting until she would call again.

"You 'wake, Johnny?"

He could smell her unpleasant night breath as she bent her head close to his.

Yawning elaborately, he turned over as if he were just awakening. "Yeah, I'm awake," he said.

"Your uncle ain't come home and it's after one o'clock . . . don't ever stay out this late . . . might have been a raid like they had last Spring. I think you better go on up there and see about him coming home. . . ."

She switched on the light and Johnny saw that she was dressed in a pink-ribboned nightgown. Her hair was down and in the soft light of the bedroom she looked very young, like a little girl, Johnny thought. One of her breasts was showing and Johnny felt a rush of hot blood rise to the top of his head.

As soon as she left him, he began to dress.

14

Out on the street, he breathed deeply of the cool night air. He was filled with a sense of adventure and was awed by the expansiveness of the darkness. The street was completely quiet and deserted and in none of the houses was there light. Despite the urgency he felt, he walked slowly, relishing the sound of his footsteps echoing between the sides of the houses. Before many minutes had passed, he turned the corner at the creek road and could see Telrico's red neon sign.

As he opened the doors, the smell of stale smoke and beer rushed out to engulf him. Right away he saw that no one was at the bar. Telrico was sitting by the stove reading a newspaper and didn't even bother to look up. Young Telrico, a thick faced youth with pimples, was sweeping the floor. He looked up as Johnny entered, and just when Johnny was about to ask him, nodded toward the back of the café.

"If you're lookin for somebody, they're all in the back."

Johnny walked toward the back room, carefully avoiding the pile of trash and sawdust heaped in the middle of the floor. The whole scene seemed part of the crazy things that were happening to him. Bill Trapp was sitting very close to his uncle with his head resting on his shoulder.

"Hello, Uncle David," Johnny said, and then, pretending he had just noticed the old white man, he said very stiffly, "And how are you, Mr. Bill?"

The two men were both very drunk. On the table before them were many empty beer bottles. The white man had unbuttoned his shirt and had one hand inside, restlessly rubbing it back and forth. His eyes, instead of being closed with drunkenness, were opened wide beyond the limits of the whites and were glazed, covered with an opaque film. His face was covered by a gratework of wrinkles. He ignored Johnny's greeting but sat with his head down, grinning, leaning all the time on Uncle David.

As Johnny stood over the dimly lit booth, his uncle rose. He smiled, swallowed the remainder of his beer, and motioned for Johnny to sit down beside him.

"He won't give me any more beer. It's after midnight he says. . . . Hell, Sam, it ain't after midnight, I've got a visitor. It ain't after midnight, Sam, it ain't after midnight yet. . . ." His voice died into a child's pleading.

15

Johnny held his breath wondering what Sam Telrico would say. Bill Trapp looked as if he were sleeping.

Without looking up from his newspaper, Telrico said, "We're closing up now, Diggs, and that's final. It's after midnight and we've got to close."

Young Telrico had stopped sweeping and was leaning on his broom, watching with frank amusement all that was going on. The way he was looking at Bill Trapp made Johnny angry and ashamed. (Look at that fart, he said to himself, I bet with all those pimples he plays with himself.)

"I guess we better be goin," Bill Trapp said, rising. "It's a nice place you have here, sir," he said, bowing from the waist to Telrico who was wrapping a scarf around his neck.

David began coughing. "All right, Johnny boy," he said when he got his breath, "we'll go home . . . go home to our little nest." Then after a moment of looking intently at Johnny's face, he said, "You sure look like her all right— you're Sis's boy all right you are. Nice boy . . . good kid. . . ."

". . . a very nice place," Bill Trapp continued, "reminds me a lot of Sid Carr's saloon in Cincinnati. Maybe they tore it down. Don't know now. Eighteen years . . . let's see . . ."

"Look, Diggs, you've got to go," Telrico shouted from behind the bar. In his dark blue overcoat he looked strangely smaller and insignificant, more like a bank clerk than a bartender now. The yellow business smile had disappeared and he seemed really irritated. "They've been makin raids," he complained, "and I ain't takin no chances on losin my license."

Bill Trapp began helping David into his coat.

"I wouldn't want them tin cops from the county to pull your license," David said, making an elegant sweeping gesture with both hands. "We're going home to our little nest, aren't we, boy? By the way, Sam, you haven't met my little nephew, have you? This is my sister's boy, Johnny, and he's staying with us while his mother's in the hospital. He's from Pittsburgh."

Sam bowed and shook hands with Johnny. "Well, sir, you're some young man now, ain't you?" he said. "Can't say he looks like you though. Lot better lookin than you are."

Johnny was pleased. He hurried to the door and held it open for Bill Trapp. He noticed how young Telrico stepped aside out of the old man's way as if he were afraid of him. Johnny fixed his eyes on the festering pimples on the youth's face; at least I don't have those, he thought to himself.

The old man leaned on Johnny for support. Johnny was surprised that he was so light. That afternoon, out on the May Farm, the old man had seemed tall and heavy, almost a giant. Now he was a weak old man and Johnny felt sorry for him.

They followed the creek road, walking in single file without speaking; sometimes the moon rode out from behind a cloud to light up the black lace pattern of bare trees that lined the bank of the creek. Sometimes the moon reflected on the top of the water shot out a single ray of light into the darkness at the bottom of the bushes.

They left Bill Trapp at the swinging bridge. "I'm much obliged to you for inviting me to the beer," he said earnestly, "much obliged." He held David by the shoulders and looked him straight in the eyes. He tweaked Johnny on the cheek and then disappeared among the blackest shadows of the bushes along the water.

"Come out and see me, come out and visit me, both of you come and see me . . ." his voice trailed away and the sound of his irregular drunken steps became fainter and fainter.

Back on their street again, they saw a light in an upstairs window of Mrs. Johnson's house.

"Must be worse, old lady Johnson," David said, stopping in front of the house. "Been saying down at the barbershop that she was in really bad shape this time."

They stood close together on the sidewalk looking up toward the window where shadows moved behind the lowered shade. Johnny felt his uncle become tense. There was something forbidding about the darkened house. One side of the roof caught the reflection of the moonlight and there was a piece of loose roofing paper that flapped with the breeze.

Johnny didn't like being on the deserted street now, especially not in front of the sick woman's house. Nor did he feel safe and secure with his uncle.

"Let's go, Uncle David," he whined, "I'm getting sleepy."

Just as they were about to enter their own door, David whispered to Johnny, "Don't bother saying anything to your Aunt Mary about Bill Trapp being there tonight."

CHAPTER THREE

T HOUGH OUTDOORS it was wet cold, her window was wide open. The curtain reached inward toward the bed where Mary was crouched under the blankets warming her hands between her thighs. She no longer was frightened. Her whole body was exhausted, not so much by the housecleaning at Pinkertons' as by the quarreling and crying. Now she waited calmly for the time when the room would be filled with the smell of onions and beer, and her husband, mumbling drunkenly to himself, would crush against her in sleep.

She had never been inside the Italian's café, but she knew everything about it from the smells her husband brought in with him. The smells and the café disgusted her and always she longed for the dawn that permitted her to leave home and husband to go to the neat, dustless whitefolks' house.

But lying there crouched with her hands warming between her legs, she longed for her husband's weight against her, not out of desire so much as out of the necessity one feels for something long known and suffered.

For almost an hour now she had been thinking about the annual Fall Festival the Missionary Guild would sponsor. Over and over again she had been telling herself there could be no foundation in what some of the ladies were saying about her being up for nomination as president of the organization in place of Mrs. Tolley who had been president almost as long as she could remember; nevertheless, the idea thrilled her. She imagined herself standing in front of the ladies presiding over a meeting. As if in shame for what she was doing, she pulled the blankets over her face to hide the grotesque expression of dignity she had shaped her face into imagining herself in a black dress saying to the ladies, "The meeting will now come to order!"

This was the true reason for her wanting the booth to be something special this year. For weeks now she had been planning its arrangement. Only after much speculation she had decided on the gingerbread idea. Only two days before her bosom friend, Helen Perkins, had asked her if she intended making more of the famous gingercake for the festival.

She pictured what the sign her husband was painting for her would look like. She imagined it in wonderful bright red, gold, and green (the colors Mrs. Pinkerton used for her paper decorations) bearing the legend: MARY'S BESTEST GINGERCAKE!

Thinking about the festival made her happy. Softly to herself under the covers, her breath feeling warm and good on her breast, she hummed a song which the evening before at choir practice they had spent almost an hour rehearsing. After a while though, the song made her sad, and feeling sorry for herself was a delicious feeling, so again she wept, silently so as not to destroy the stillness. She sobbed until from down the street, she heard footsteps and soft talking. This must be them! She jumped out of bed then and ran to the bathroom where she splashed cold water on her face.

PART TWO

■ CHAPTER ONE

A BRISK COLD wind blew down the street from the creek chasing leaves and candy wrappers before it. Frantic birds flocked above and behind the wind, riding the violent currents, screaming, overloading trees. A fat tomcat, sooty gray like the sky, was sitting on the steps of the barbershop when Johnny arrived. It didn't flee or move aside but sat looking at him brazenly as if to question his right to enter. Although it was already after nine o'clock, the weak morning light made it seem much earlier.

Opening the door of the shop (which was really a built-over streetcar of the ancient type used by the city when buses were put on), Johnny was surprised that there was already a group of men sitting on the waiting chairs. Both barber chairs were unoccupied although one was piled high with dirty linen. The floor was covered with tiny hair balls and cigarette butts.

"Yes sir?" Tolley said, laboriously rising out of a chair in the corner. "Sit down there in the chair, sonny, and we'll get at you." He had a high, reedy voice that eased out of his tiny, thick lips like a whistle. He was a fat man whose extra wide fireman's suspenders defined the shape of his body in a grand arc that reached an apex at the bottom button of his vest.

"Just a haircut," Johnny said. He wondered how the barber would be able to cut his hair when his belly poked so far in front of him and his arms were so short. While the barber tucked a raggedy sheet around his neck, Johnny had a chance to look around at the other men seated in a row on the theater chairs reserved for waiting customers.

All of them stared at Johnny, none of them moving, apparently not breathing. One of them, a boy of about sixteen with a football shaped head piled high with heavily greased hair, held a shoe in one hand and a brush poised in the other.

23

Only then did Johnny realize that he was the focus of attention.

"You the boy stayin with Diggs?" Tolley asked.

"Yessir. I'm their nephew."

"He's Diggs' nephew, stayin with them," Tolley explained, turning toward the others as if they hadn't heard, adding, "He's from *Pittsburgh*."

"Pittsburgh, huh? The Smokey City . . . was in Pittsburgh in nineteen-thirty. North Side . . . Green Street. . . ."

Johnny twisted his head from out of the vise-like grip of the barber to look through the mirror at the man who was speaking.

He was a sly looking man with a wooden leg which lay unstrapped behind him against the wall. Johnny could see five very large discolored teeth, so well spaced, that counting them was inevitable. His skin was a deep pigmented yellow and slightly greasy on the cheeks. He held what looked like a notebook in his hand and behind his ear, almost hidden by thick, gray hair, was a bright yellow pencil.

"Hee, hee, hee! You be the boy that old white man caught up his apple tree, ain't you?"

Johnny felt his neck becoming hot with shame. The sheet became intolerably sticky. Without looking, he knew to whom the hoarse, whispering voice belonged. It was a withered, skull-head of a man seated near the door. He was dressed in a black suit of heavy material and wore a gold Elk chain that swung down the front of his vest.

Johnny closed his eyes, pretending he couldn't hear.

"Yeah, he's the one all right," the shoeshine boy said triumphantly. He began to giggle uncontrollably. . . . "He's the one, he's the one. . . ."

"Well the boy didn't know, Bill," Tolley said. "Can't be blamed. . . ."

"Yeah, but just the same, ought to be careful," the one-legged man, who was called Slim, said. "Never can tell what a crazy son-of-a-beehive like him'll do."

"That time Mrs. Green and them ladies went out there, five or six years back, and he chased them off the place . . ." Tolley's voice died away in a thin whistle as he maneuvered the clippers over the top of Johnny's head.

Jim Anderson, the skull-headed gentleman, polished his

cane with a handkerchief. "Well, sir, he sure is one strange white man. . . ."

"Must got a lot of money," Slim said. "Must have—else he'd have to work or something. . . ."

"Oh, I don't know," Tolley said. "There's lots of them white folks got ways of gettin money. Don't have to work so hard. Lots of them's thrifty and don't throw their money away like our folks do."

"That's a fact," Slim said. "That time young Wilson hit for two hundred, didn't have a cent of it two weeks later. Our folks just don't know how to do when it comes to money."

"Might not be such a bad egg," Tolley said. "Diggs was telling me that he was treated very nice by the white man when he went out to rescue the boy here. Ain't that right, sonny?"

Johnny kept his head lowered. He didn't want to see the others looking at him with those appraising eyes as if they were just waiting for him to say something to make them laugh.

"Well, he didn't do nothing to me; he's a very nice man."

"S'wonder he didn't shoot at you with that gun a his," said Bill, the shoeshine boy. "I seen it. It's a Winchester, a beauty."

"Well, you can't tell what kind a man is just by lookin on the outside. Used to cut hair for an old white man for fifteen years solid. Thought he was about the worst evil tempered white man I ever seen. One day he comes just like he always did to get his hair cut—just before Christmas it was—and slipped me a fifty-dollar bill. Back in them days, fifty dollars was worth lots more than it is today."

"I remember a white man once used to come and play one cent every day on two-o-two, regular as a clock, every morning—two-o-two. This was in good times, around twenty-eight, down Fairmont. Funny old bird. Some kind of hunky looked like, dressed in rags most of the time. Well, sir—one day he don't come. That night I hears he done dropped dead on the street. And would you believe it, they found almost ten thousand dollars in that old bird's mattress. . . . Yessirree! Ten thousand smackers of Uncle's Sam's greenbacks."

"Don't suppose that Bill Trapp got a lot of money hid out there somewhere, do you?" Tolley asked.

WILLIAM DEMBY

"Well, you'd never catch me going out there," Bill, the shoeshine boy, said, rolling his eyes upward in an idiotic grimace. "Went past there one night on my way back from Grady Mine. Had to cut past there near his fence and saw these here fizzlin lights. Hear someone singing weirdest old songs I ever heard. Man-n, I whipped out a there. Yeah man, I *sure* whipped out of there. I wouldn't care if he got twenty thousand dollars hid under his mattress."

And Bill rolled his eyes and threw his head back and laughed and laughed, shaking all over, until he had to hold onto his shoeshine stand for support.

"He *do* have funny eyes," Jim Anderson said. "I passed him on the street once. Said hideedoo, but he just looked and grunted somethin or other. 'Nough to make a man want to run away from those eyes. . . ."

"Well, if he *do* have money," Slim said, "I sure would like to get my hand on some. Ain't had a hit in two weeks."

"How do you want it cut on the sides, sonny? Pretty boy like you ought to have nice long sideburns. That's the way the gals like them." Tolley began giggling, and again Johnny felt hot shame under his collar. He wished the fat old fool would hurry and finish.

Uncle David came in the barbershop carrying the box that contained his brushes and paints.

"Gentlemen," he greeted. Then, spying Johnny, he said, "Getting all slicked up, huh?"

"Howdy, Diggs," Tolley said, waving the lather covered razor in his direction.

"Goin out to make all that money," Slim said, "better stop here and see me. Got a feelin you might catch him today."

"Well, I don't know," David said, reaching into his pocket, a serious expression on his face. "Might play six-six-seven in the box for a penny. Might be my lucky day," he added wistfully.

"Give me a penny boxed on six-six-seven," said Jim Anderson. "Used to be my boss's telephone number back in nineteen twenty—six-six-seven-zero. Funny how those numbers come back to you, remember when . . ."

"Now don't crowd me now, Jim," Slim said. "You been sittin there all morning and ain't thought about playing till

26

Diggs comes in. Give him a chance, he's got a job, and Lord knows that don't happen any too often."

"You got a new job this mornin?" Tolley asked.

"Sign for Newman's Furs. Hank Ellis got it for me," David answered.

"You make pretty good now?"

"Don't pay what it used to, but it's something."

"Don't many of our folks got skill to paint signs," Jim Anderson said.

"Used to be one down Fairmont got rich painting signs, colored man named Herberts, way before they filled in the dam. He's gone to Pittsburgh now." Tolley was dusting Johnny with powder. He had already sprinkled his head with the sticky, too sweet smelling lavender water that always reminded him of the mixed smells of the five and ten cent stores.

"Sit down, Johnny, I'll be going myself in a minute," Uncle David said, seating himself in the only vacant barber chair.

Johnny found a seat on a box near the stove. When he passed, his uncle pinched his behind. This made Johnny angry and he hoped the shoeshine boy wasn't looking.

Tolley was sitting in the corner on a tiny stool, changing his street shoes for the tennis shoes he regularly wore in the shop.

"Be with you in just a minute, Diggs," he said.

Slim wrote the numbers down in his little receipt book. Before each entry, as if to see better, he would bite the end of the pencil and narrow his eyes. He took a battered pair of spectacles that were held together by wire and put them on so that they hung near the tip of his nose. Johnny could hardly keep his eyes off the wooden leg leaning against the wall or from the stub where the trouser, shiny and bright compared with the faded trouser of the good leg, was rolled up in a neat bundle.

"Hear tell you and that old white man out there on the May place gettin to be right good friends," Slim said cunningly. "Tell me you even bringin him down to Telrico's sometime?"

The shoeshine boy stopped brushing a shoe. Tolley hurriedly tied his other shoe and wobbled over to the chair so

27

he could be nearer the conversation. The shop became very quiet and Johnny wondered what was going to happen.

"Well, naturally I went out there when I found out the man picked up the kid here. You would of done the same."

Slim counted the change very slowly as if he weren't really interested in what David was saying. David, accepting the change, counted it equally as slowly.

"What's the old bird like?" Slim asked, stuffing his notebook into his hip pocket.

"That's right," Tolley said; "you about the first one around here to get close enough to the man to say boo to him."

"Ain't nothing much to tell," David said, trying to yawn. "Soon as those kids come running into Telrico's yelling that the old man caught the boy here, I went a running. Just like I told you before, whenever I got there, there was Johnny sitting on the man's porch, chatting away like he'd been friends with him always. Naturally I shot off the mouth about what's he mean bothering the kids and all, but what does he do but go in the house and bring out a big bottle of wine and tells me to take a drink. We got to drinking and talking and I just forgot why I went out there in the first place."

"Well, sir. I've got to give it to you," Tolley said. "You the first one in all these years."

"I talked with him," David continued, "and he seemed like an intelligent white man."

"If you mean that peckerwood's got the same ideas you got," Slim said, "you're both of you losing your mind."

"I wouldn't trust a white sonuvabitch as far as I could spit!" said Bill, the shoeshine boy.

"Well, to tell you the truth, I didn't ever think there was anything really wrong with him. Used to walk past here on his way uptown sometimes and far as I could see, he was all right." Tolley returned to his chair and sat facing the window.

"Well, I ain't seen him face to face except once I passed him on the swinging bridge and I mean to tell you there's something mighty funny about him." Slim rubbed the stump of his leg.

"I wouldn't trust a white man further than I could spit— they'll grin in your face and rub your hair, but just you turn your back . . ." Bill cut his throat with an imaginary knife.

Tolley pouted his little round lips. "It's all right for that brotherly love talk of yours in church, Diggs, but when you get down to brass tacks, brother, you got to fight fire with fire."

"Now you take a white man like that been livin out there in the woods there for goin on fifteen years don't say nothin to nobody, now if that ain't prejudiss, I want to know what is." Jim Anderson had moved closer to David and was talking right into his face. "Somethin mighty funny about a white man livin round darkies when he got good places over there in the white part of town. Don't make sense, must got somethin up his sleeve."

At that moment the door opened and a small, thin man with an almost perfectly round head entered the door. He wore a dark blue suit and a black tie that was tied in a tiny knot that fit with incredible precision into the appointed vertex of a stiff, starched collar.

"Well, I suppose you've heard the news, gentlemen?" He spoke without dialect in an affected manner, separating each word like a high school English teacher.

"Morning, Reverend," the chorus greeted.

"Sister Johnson is much worse, much worse indeed. In fact, brothers, she isn't expected to live through the night." He smiled broadly and turned from one face to the other. He raised a hand in blessing and smiled a gold sprinkled smile as if he were imparting good news.

"Well, it sure is too bad, I suppose, ailin all these years, really suffering poor soul, I guess it's all for the best." Tolley stood with his hands to his sides, a sorrowful expression on his face.

"Yes. I suppose one could say that it is a wonderful manifestation of His Divine Love that her suffering will soon come to an end and she will be embraced in the Heavenly Kingdom." The Reverend bowed his head in silent meditation. The barbershop, for a moment, was quiet. Then he coughed and sat himself on the stool the shoeshine boy vacated for him. He put two small yellow slippers covered by spats on the footrest and looked at them critically as Bill began to dust them.

"Sister Johnson has been in great pain," he added.

"Poor soul's been alone all these years, all by herself," Jim Anderson said, rubbing his cheek thoughtfully. "Don't suppose that girl a her's comin home now, do you?"

"Well, as a matter of fact, we've wired the daughter, informing her of her mother's condition and urging her to come home as soon as possible." The Reverend had a booming voice that echoed around the shop.

"S'bout time she comin home," Slim said.

"That's one wild gal," Bill said. "That sure is one wild gal from what they tell me."

"Used to be a nice girl, that Edith. As I remember, used to be a sweetie of yours, wasn't she, Diggs?" Tolley looked over toward David who was looking out the window.

Johnny wondered if the girl looked like a beautiful colored girl he saw in the movies once.

"Well, college changes the best of them," Slim said. "There she is going to ruin up there in the city with all her book learnin. It's nothing but a waste of money to send them to college."

"She has had every chance that girl has, and it isn't the Lord's fault that she hasn't availed herself of that which He has so abundantly placed in her hands."

"Well, I know one thing," Jim Anderson said, "them adopted kids sure do some funny things. I remember my aunt's nephew ran away with her insurance money and done spent half of it before they ever did miss it."

"S'bad blood in them adopted kids makes them like that," Slim said. "I'd think twice before I ever adopted me one."

"Don't understand why she ever did a thing like that. That girl had everything she wanted. . . ."

"Yes, Mrs. Johnson must have made pretty good with that pension and her dressmaking."

"Mrs. Johnson made right smart, all right," Slim said, "but it weren't enough for that gal. Beetlecreek wasn't good enough for her, she had to go and head for the big city."

"Let us hope that her mother's grave condition will make her repent of her sins and once again put her feet on the straight and narrow path to Divine Grace." The Reverend fingered the brass cross he wore on his lapel and licked his lips.

Then there was silence again. Tolley, breathing heavily from the morning's exertion, fanned himself with a calendar.

"Sister Johnson has done a lot of work for the church. If worst comes to worst . . ."

"I'll start takin up a collection for a fine floral piece," Slim said.

"We never know what His plans for us are . . . we know not the hour or the day . . ."

"Come on, Johnny," David whispered, rising, "let's get out of here."

"You going already, Diggs? Well, now, you get all yo peckerwood friends together and we'll have us a meeting on brotherly love." And Slim broke out into a side-mouth, hissing laugh. Bill the shoeshine boy joined him and looked right into Johnny's face and began laughing even louder so that drops of spittle flew into Johnny's face.

Involuntarily, Johnny threw his hands up to protect his face and hurried out the door. In the street he could still hear the chorus of laughter and the stomping of feet.

"Bunch a damn fool darkies," David said as soon as they were on the street. "Bunch of damn fools!" But he looked toward the window as if he were afraid they had heard him. "Take that Slim now. He's got all that money and all he thinks about is making more."

Johnny rubbed the back of his head. The barber had cut his hair so close that the lump on the back of his head was as smooth as his cheek. Coming from a barber always made him feel ashamed. It was just like the first time he wore long trousers to church, like expecting everyone he met to talk about him after he had passed. He felt naked, as if his whole physical appearance were thrown out of proportion, as if with his hair shorter, his nose had become longer and his nostrils wider. He wished he had brought his hat, or better still, owned a cap like the boys in the gang all wore.

"You going to work?" he asked of his uncle.

"Just going to paint this here sign. You can come if you want to."

"No. I better not," Johnny answered quickly. "Better not, because I promised Aunt Mary I'd come right home."

"Well, tell your Aunt Mary I'll be home late for lunch. God knows when I'll finish this sign."

Johnny watched his uncle until he disappeared around the corner at the railroad crossing. He felt free at last and knew

31

that he wouldn't go home but would head toward the swinging bridge where the gang was probably playing or fooling around. It was Saturday and there would be no school.

He took a handful of pebbl   and ran along the dusty road throwing them at the street light. He passed two women and a little girl and said, Howdeedoo, to them.

As soon as he had passed them, he heard the oldest and the fattest of the two ladies say, "That's the boy from Pittsburgh who's stayin at the Diggses," adding in an awe-struck voice, "He's the one that old white man caught up the tree."

And Johnny, without turning his head, knew that the women were looking at him, that they had stopped in the road and were examining him with their funny, squinchy-eyed way of looking. He straightened his shoulders and walked along the road, taking what he thought were long, athletic strides, whistling very loudly a marching song. He was a hero, an important personage, and this was a new feeling for him and it made him very happy.

■ CHAPTER TWO

THEY pretended they didn't see him when he walked over to the railing of the bridge. They were standing slouched and posed with their hands in their pockets, smoking in rotation a short, wet cigarette butt.

"Hiya, Pittsburgh Kid!" Baby Boy was the first one to speak. He put his arm around Johnny's shoulder and steered him toward the rest of the boys. Johnny was grateful for Baby Boy's attention.

The Leader had his back toward Johnny and was busy chipping hunks of wood from the railing.

"Hello, fellows," Johnny said. He tried to make himself sound casual, but he realized right away that his voice was quivering. He took a tennis ball from his pocket and began bouncing it as if it were a basketball.

No one answered his greeting although all of them except the Leader grunted or hunched their shoulders in way of response. But, in spite of all this, Johnny could tell by the way the other two boys stole looks at him from the corners of their lowered eyes, that he had won new respect from them because of what had happened at Bill Trapp's.

"I saw you and yo uncle last night," the Leader said, a wry smile barely concealing the nervousness revealed in his sleepy eyes. "That fart of yours sure was drunk, must of een nursed on a bottle."

The Leader hoisted up his trousers and pulled on the rayed red suspender that was hanging from his shoulder. As if this were a signal, a titter circled the group and rescendoed into uncontrolled laughter. Only Baby Boy and ohnny didn't laugh.

Johnny felt the very same stabbing fears and embarrassments he had felt almost two weeks before, when he first encountered the gang. He could think of nothing to say that would belittle them. He hated and at the same time envied the Leader for his way of leaning back rocking on his heels with his thumb in the red suspenders. Even the thought that they were down-home boys and he was from the big city didn't comfort him.

The Leader was standing so close, Johnny could feel the rise and fall of his stomach against his own. There was a sickening, sour milk smell about him.

Finally, Baby Boy asked, "What about it, Johnny? What'd he do to you?"

"Oh, it wasn't nothing. . . ."

There was a hole in the bottom plank of the bridge and in it was a waxy beetle struggling to get off its back. He took the beetle, and turning so they couldn't see him, he placed it carefully on the leaf of a bush.

"If you wouldn't of been so slow, you could of got away easy," the Leader said, looking from one boy's face to the other as if seeking confirmation in their expressions.

"He didn't do nothing," Johnny said. "Took me to the house and gave me cider, that's all."

He was angry with himself. This wasn't what he wanted to say at all. He had planned an entirely different story, a more exciting story that would give him more heroic importance.

The Leader sat on the railing and the other boys followed his example until there was only Johnny standing in the middle of the bridge.

"At first I was scared . . . he sure is a fearsome guy . . looked at me with those funny eyes . . . I didn't know what he was going to do."

Johnny couldn't continue. Everything he had planned to say escaped his memory just like the time he had a Christmas recitation to say and he hadn't been able to remember whether he was supposed to say, Hail the new born King, or, Hail, the King is born.

He took the tennis ball and threw it high in the air and clapped his hands once before catching it.

"What do you say we go to the shanty," Baby Boy said.

"D'you want to go to the shanty?" the Leader asked Johnny

"Sure," Johnny said. They had never invited him before and he felt a little nervous.

They walked to the end of the bridge on the same side of the railroad tracks and climbed down through a path under a small trestle where the creek had backed up to form a small pond. On the side of the pond nearest the pillars of the trestle, in fact, nailed to the trestle, was a small shanty with a sloping, tar paper roof partly hidden by low hanging branches of a wild cherry tree.

"Hotdiggedy!" Johnny exclaimed.

The boys, all smiling proudly, made room for him while he pushed through the bushes in front of the doorway. He was about to open the door when the Leader stopped him.

"Wait a minute, boy! Don't just anybody go in there. This here's a secret place. You only go in there if you're a member or a guest."

"What is it, a club?"

The only club to which Johnny had ever belonged was the Civics Club in school.

"S'a secret society," Baby Boy whispered.

"We's the Nightriders," one of the other two boys who up to now had remained silent, said. He had a long, red scaly neck.

"Well, how about it?" insisted the Leader, "you want to join or don't you?"

Johnny didn't know what to say. This was more than he had hoped for. They were really asking him to join their club!

"Sure, I'll join," Johnny stammered rather too eagerly, "what do I have to do?"

"You'll be initiated," Baby Boy whispered to him excitedly.

It was too dark to see anything at first, but the Leader struck a match and lit a lantern that swung from the ceiling. The room was larger than it appeared from outside. Johnny liked the fetid, closed-in smell of the room, a smell like that of a moldy, damp pocketbook he had once found under his back porch.

When his eyes became accustomed to the dark, he saw that the walls were covered with pictures torn from magazines. Some of the pictures were of baseball players and orchestra leaders, but most of them were photographs of movie actresses in bathing suits.

"C'mere. Look at this," the Leader said. And he steered Johnny to a corner where there was what appeared to be kind of curtain tacked to the wall. The other four boys gathered around.

He pulled the curtain aside. "Look at these farts," he said. And there, pasted to the wall, were pictures cut from pornographic cartoon book.

Johnny felt a wave of heat tear at his stomach muscles. He wanted to turn his head away in disgust, at the same time wanted very much to look and look at the wonderful pictures of things he had never seen before. He was afraid that if he tried to say anything, he would be unable to make sound.

Baby Boy, who was standing behind him, was hopping up and down in a kind of dance, his hands between his legs. "Woo, woo!" he shouted, all the while giggling.

The red-necked boy had his hands in his pockets and was rubbing them back and forth nervously, at the same time he shimmied up and down the floor.

"I bet you can't even dog-water," said one of the other boys who was seated in a dark corner.

Johnny turned his head and saw what the boy was doing. He wanted to run away from the terrible shack and the terrible boys. Their fingernails will fall out and their teeth, he mumbled to himself. But he remembered his own sins and this made him even more ashamed. Quickly he turned his head so that he wouldn't have to look at them or say anything—most of all he feared their laughter and ridicule. Only this fear kept him from running out the door.

He turned his back toward them and began leafing through a sport magazine, hoping in this way to calm himself. He could hear their heavy breathing and occasional gasps of high pitched laughter. He fought an almost overwhelming desire to go to the corner to look at the pictures again. He kept seeing one picture in particular, Little Orphan Annie in the embrace of Punjab.

After a while, the boys pulled out cigarette butts and began to pass them around.

"You want to smoke?" Baby Boy asked Johnny.

Johnny had never smoked before; once he had started to smoke a cornsilk cigarette but the odor had made him sick

"Well . . . I don't know . . . maybe I better not. I got a sore throat."

But when he saw the amused looks the others were giving him, he accepted the brown-stained butt the boy was handing him and gingerly put it in his mouth. He kept his lips as dry as possible because he knew Baby Boy hadn't washed his hands after what he had just done.

They were all sitting on the floor with their backs to the wall. Baby Boy was half leaning on Johnny's shoulder while the Leader told them a dirty joke:

". . . and when the fart jumped in with her, he found out hers was bigger than his!"

Johnny joined in the laughter but he didn't see anything funny in the joke. He was panic-stricken when Baby Boy asked him to tell one. The only joke he knew had to do with a school teacher who found out that her pupil had put catsup in the inkwell, but it wasn't a dirty joke at all.

A frightened baby pigeon flew into the room through the small window and zipped back and forth over their heads and against the floor and ceiling.

Johnny reached out his hand and tried to catch it. So did the other boys, but the crazy bird was not to be caught. They ran back and forth through the narrow space, stumbling over each other, screaming with excitement.

"Whoo-whoo! Little fart . . . h'ya is . . . whoo-whoo! Now I's got ya. . . ."

Until finally Johnny caught the bird, trapped him in the corner where the ceiling was low, and cupped his hands over the soft, trembling wings and held it firm. Birds reminded Johnny of feeling sorry for animals and he caressed the warm, pulsating softness. He was about to set the bird free, when the Leader snatched it from his hands.

"Don't! You'll hurt it," Johnny exclaimed. He saw the red, glassy eyes of the bird and how strangely they contrasted with the purple head.

The Leader took the bleating bird by the neck and began to swing it over his head in an ever increasing arc. Johnny watched horrified as drops of blood sprinkled the floor. Suddenly the body was torn from the head and smashed against the wall with a loud thud.

The Leader's eyes were shining and his mouth was open in a toothy, insane grin. For a moment he kept looking at the

37

spot where the bird's body had struck the wall, then, realizing that he still held the bloody fragment of the bird's head in his hand, he burst out laughing and all the boys began to laugh—all except Johnny.

Johnny felt sick in the stomach and was afraid he would vomit. Suddenly, the Leader ran at Johnny, thrusting the bloody bird head in Johnny's face. Johnny became pale— frozen with fright. He couldn't get his breath.

With all the strength that remained, he kept himself from breaking out in tears. "I'll see you guys," he said, and he walked out the door.

No one said anything. Johnny wouldn't look at them but when he was out on the railroad tracks, he heard a single voice laughing.

There was a purple and gray feather on his shirt. He took the feather and rubbed it between his fingers and then put it up to his nose to smell, but there was no odor.

Johnny was afraid and he was very sad. He crossed the swinging bridge and began walking aimlessly along the creek road away from the village. He didn't want to go home, it was still too early for lunch. Besides he wanted to be alone.

Once his mother had appeared suddenly in the bathroom while he was taking a bath and had warned him against doing the devil's work. She had shown him a picture in a large, leather covered doctor's book, of a boy with a huge head and popping eyes, one of which was blind. The boy was bald and his face was covered with hideous sores. "This is what will happen to you," she said. And this, he had never forgotten, and always afterward he would pray fervently for God to forgive him, and he couldn't face anyone, and every day he would check his face for signs of change.

He was sorry to have seen what he had seen, sorry to have felt what he had felt. Because, before, it had been a secret sin. He was alone, the only sinner, and as such, could bear his sin. But to see it in others—to have seen what the boys were doing—was like telling the world of his own sin.

The baby pigeon that had flown into the room was a soft little bird and he had felt sorry for it. His instinct had been to protect it, but the Leader had swung it round and round over his head until the body was separated from the head, till blood dropped to the floor, till purple and gray feathers

38

drifted gently as in a dream through the air, until the bleating had stopped. And he knew that, behind the terror and the feeling sorry for the bird, the dead creature, was also a new feeling: a new feeling of envy for the power the Leader had over things and creatures and the other boys, power and contempt, a certain hardness that he, Johnny, had never had but which he recognized now as an important thing. And Johnny, walking along the creek road, puzzled and pondered over these thoughts, all the while rubbing the piece of leather between his fingers.

■ CHAPTER THREE

Now the days were long; time moved slowly for Bil
Trapp. Every morning found him up and about long before dawn. He was restless and spent his time doing un
necessary things; he mended traps and pruned trees, working
always near the road, hoping to see the colored boy, hoping
to see any human walking toward his place. One day, a
colored lady pushing a wheelbarrow of ashes passed on the
road. He stopped working to watch her broad behind disap
pear around the bend of the road. Every evening as soon a
the sun had set he would begin drinking. This he did to
hasten the passing of night. His sleep then would be heavy
only toward morning, just before dawn, would he dream
Once he dreamed of a gigantic circus tent that stretched as
far as the eye could see. Dressed in the fancy military uni
form, holding the torches, he stood in the very middle o
the circular stage; all around him were thousands and thou
sands of children who applauded and screamed as he waved
the torches in the air.

Sometimes in the morning, feeling safe in the sweaty
warmth of the blankets, he would try to think back to the
days when he was with Harry Simcoe's Continental Show
Almost always then his thoughts would cluster about a cer
tain smell, a feeling connected with the carnival. Most of the
time he would think of the place behind Mr. Stein's ten
where everyone went to pass their water.

He used to stand there in the darkness behind that ten
resigned and happy to be there, straddling the puddle of hi
own steaming urine. No matter where they were—Martins

40

ville, Harperstown, Mansfield, Braddock, Cleveland—the puddle was always the same, a tiny lake of steaming lava in the sand or sawdust. The patched piece of canvas on the back wall of the tent, as well as the frayed piece of rope looped three times around the tent peg, were always there to fix the gaze upon. In a time when his life was made up of moving about through strange town landscapes, this place behind Mr. Stein's tent where everyone came to do it remained fixed and unchangeable. Dogs sniffed happily around this place.

As soon as he finished unpacking the prizes on nights he didn't have anything else to do, he would rush there to stand quietly while thoughts of the past would rise up out of the steam.

He would try to think of being a child; he would try to recreate the picture of him and Hilda saying their prayers together while Mrs. Haines stood there behind them, her heavy asthmatic breathing filling in the spaces between the rushed syllables of "Now I laymee. . . ." Then, just thinking of the name, Mrs. Haines, made him remember the shame he used to feel of being an adopted child, made him remember how sorry he felt for her having an ugly child like him on her hands, though, when some of the children at school told him she got money from the county for taking care of them, he felt better.

As a child, almost every thought he had was conditioned by his ugliness, and even as an adult, long after Mrs. Haines was dead and Hilda and he had no one but themselves, he would blush with terrible embarrassment for his sister whenever anyone would remark how much they resembled one another. He expected very little from people. He was rather ashamed to be in the world and claimed few rights for himself. Outside of him was Hilda upon whose love he could count, though even this love he accepted gingerly, hardly daring to believe it real.

When Mrs. Haines died, they both left school to take jobs, he in a blacksmith shop which later became a garage, and Hilda as a maid in a ladies' boarding house. Every Saturday night he would take half of his pay to her, stopping first to buy two pints of ice cream and a fifteen cent cake which gravely they would eat sitting on the back steps. Then, when they had finished and washed their hands, she would tell him that they must save their money so that some day they could live as respectable people should. Twenty years passed before they knew it. Twice during that time the price of ice cream changed.

The garage where he worked closed down one winter and he took a job as handyman with a carnival that happened to be passing through. Hilda left the town that same winter to take up residence in a ladies' boarding house in a nearby town. There she did needle work and lived from the money she had saved.

Now he could only visit his sister twice a year, once in the winter and once in the late spring. He still took presents with him when he went to visit her, usually a souvenir basket of fruit from California wrapped in real silk ribbons. She would place the gift down on the table, pretending to ignore it, and immediately start giving him a tongue lashing. "Why you want to waste away your life running around the country with a carnival is more than I can see," she would say, her long nose twitching and her hands imploring the air. "We're respectable folks but *you* don't seem to care anything about my reputation." He would sit there on the stiff-backed chair trying to keep from touching with his back the doily she'd stitched herself. When she would finish and he'd finished the tea she always served him in tiny fragile cups, he would leave filled with the conviction that she was right and that he must do something about his life.

It was after one of these visits that he decided to take up the Retirement Plan Insurance. All the week before he kept seeing the picture of the Happy Man and Cottage in the back pages of the western magazine they used for toilet paper in the portable latrine. At first he tried to ignore the picture but always, thinking of what his sister had told him, the picture would come back to his mind. Once, unable to ignore the call any longer, he went into the toilet and took the magazine to his tent and filled out the coupon. When the important looking envelope filled with pink forms arrived, he felt very excited, almost as if he was taking his first communion.

Carefully he filled out the forms and when they were safely in the mail, he wrote a long letter to his sister telling her in the same words of the advertisement just what the Retirement Plan Insurance was. She thought it was a splendid idea and told him again of how they came from respectable

42

folks, and that he owed it to the memory of their folks to try to better himself. He was past forty then, but the insurance made him feel much younger.

Hilda died of pneumonia soon after he began the Retirement Plan Insurance. Mr. Stein gave him two days off to go to the funeral. He didn't know any of the ladies dressed in black and navy blue who cried at the funeral and was ashamed to make himself known to them. As soon as it was over, he slipped away unnoticed and decided to go to Niagara Falls where he had never been before.

He waited until the guide took the group back down for the trip under the falls and stood all alone there at the railing, while the roar of the water blasted away his identity. Then, with the perfumed memory of the pretty funeral and flowers Hilda had had combined in his mind with the feeling of being on a kind of vacation, his first, he began to cry out of joy. For the first time in his life he almost understood something. He wasn't ashamed. On his way back to the bus stop he stopped in a roadhouse to have a beer. For once he felt like respectable folks and even put money in the music box.

He didn't take up with the Italian at once; a year of gray-passing time went by and he no longer sent money to the Retirement Plan. The envelopes which kept coming he placed in a neat pile on his washstand box where the wind blowing through the tent kept them free from dust. Hair began growing on his soul. Never before in his life had he been without someone who could confirm his own existence, into whose life he could sometime look.

But one rainy night he was standing behind the money-counting tent watching the slow, cheap bracelet swinging of the ferris wheel when the Italian appeared there behind him. "You've been standing there a long time," the Italian said.

He should have been ashamed but he wasn't. He stood aside for the Italian, but instead the Italian accompanied him back to the street. "My dog's sick," he said, "it's the rain and this food. . . ." Bill Trapp was glad that it was dark and misty and that he couldn't see the Italian's face; it sounded as if he were crying.

Although he had seen the Italian many times, he had never spoken one word to him. The Italian was a performer, though

43

a shabby one in ill repute with the flashier performers, and he was only a handyman; but it wasn't that that kept them apart. The Italian drank constantly and this as much as his own shyness kept him from ever doing more than to nod in passing. But this time he went with him to look at the dog, an aged hound with long shiny hair and a face like an old complaining woman. From that day on, he and the Italian became friends.

The Italian gave him a costume, the uniform of an old Corsican cavalier, and allowed him to participate in the dog act. All Bill Trapp had to do was to hold a flaming torch that changed colors as different powders burned throughout the entire act, while the dogs "talked," rolled over, counted, and played dead. They don't understand theater, these American audiences, the Italian would complain after every act.

Bill Trapp knew that their friendship obviously depended on the fact that he was the only one who would listen to the Italian's drunken conversations, but just as when he was a child he used to accept the other children's taunts willingly if it meant some kind of recognition for himself, he now accepted the Italian's abuse. Every time they came to a new town, as soon as he had tied up the last loop around headquarters tent, he would hurry uptown to buy a bottle of cheap liquor to give the Italian. He would hurry through his supper then (the Italian insisted on eating alone in his tent with the dogs) and afterwards, cleanly shaven, would make his call on the Italian.

During those years, he was almost happy. There was a kind of order to his life that hadn't been before, and every evening he could count on listening to the Italian complain about the world. His soul became alive again and the possibility of a future became real to him. He told the Italian about the Retirement Insurance Plan but the Italian only laughed at him, saying that the only true investment was the investment of the mind. Soon afterwards they sent away for a set of books, *The Facts of Life Series*: A Compilation of all the World's Knowledge with Particular Emphasis on the Wonderful Mysteries of the Human Machine. Though it was mostly his money that was sent, he didn't mind, because he spent little money for himself and had never touched the money he'd begun saving when he first began working.

First the Italian's dog died and then the Italian himself.

When the dog died, the Italian took the body to a taxidermist and left it there to be stuffed. He didn't go to get the dog till a week later when they'd already moved to another town. He disappeared for almost a week and everyone had given him up for good. ("Good riddance," said Mr. Stein, who'd kept the Italian and the dog act just because the Italian had once been such a famous trapeze artist.) Bill Trapp held tight inside himself and wouldn't let himself feel anything. He took to standing a long time at the urine puddle again. Then one night, standing there thinking soft fuzzy balls of thoughts, he saw the Italian enter the tent. He was covered with mud and his eyes were pus-filled but he carried the oily stuffed dog in his arms. He wouldn't speak to Bill Trapp when he went into the tent; he just lay there looking a hole through the ceiling. The new books were covered with toothpaste and spoiled food and they sometimes used them to sit on. A bottle of sour milk stunk up the close atmosphere inside the tent. That same night the Italian died.

No one knew what to do with the stuffed dog. Bill Trapp didn't want it. He wouldn't accept anything that had belonged to the Italian except the uniform, some of the fire powder that he used in the torches, and the books. The only real regret he had was that he could no longer dress up and participate in the dog act. Standing there before the people, especially the children, he had felt important, belonging to the world, worth while and unashamed. Now that would be no more. As far as the Italian's death, he had become used to the necessity of death, and now decided to wait peaceably for his own. He suddenly felt like an old man. He had been a child once, now he was an old man. There had been no middle period of youth.

The County took the body away and that was the end for Bill Trapp and the carnival. They were in Ridgeville then and when he saw the farm known as the May Place there between the Negro part of town and the white business section, he made up his mind to buy it and live there the rest of his life. Way in the back of his mind was the picture of the Happy Man and Cottage of the Retirement Plan.

One more night, for the last time, he straddled the puddle of his own steaming urine, and, just as at Niagara Falls that day, he came close to understanding something, he came close to understanding why it was that he had never lived, why it was that his life had been incomplete, only half tasted; he understood (though vaguely, without the thoughts taking the form of words or ideas) the necessity of giving himself the right and power to reach out and touch people, to love. He blamed no one for the shriveled paleness of his soul. But now it was too late. All these years he had waited for the touch, the gesture, from others fearing to make the gesture, the touch, himself for fear of being rebuffed. He kicked a pile of sawdust into the puddle then and left the carnival. Ten years had gone by.

Negroes passed back and forth to see him move into the May Place. All that week, while he cut grass and made the shanty livable, they moved back and forth restlessly on the road.

Mr. Stein had never hired Negroes for the carnival, but they were always the first to begin hanging around whenever the big tents went up. In the afternoon, in the dust and direct heat, whenever the white people were all indoors, there would still be Negroes shuffling through the sawdust picking up bits of paper to look at, kicking at tent pegs. Sometimes they would sit in the shade and he would hear them talking softly like church whispering. From the slit in the corner of his tent, he would watch them. Even from that distance, he felt close to them. Watching them secretly as he did he could see that they were always dodging something, were ashamed of something just as he was; they were the same breed as he. Still, whenever they would stand behind him while he hammered down the stakes and he would feel their cue-ball eyes measuring his back, his hands would sweat with something akin to fear. Sometimes he would miss a stroke and wonder if they were winking at each other, making their secret jokes there behind his back.

He began to think about that colored boy, Johnny, and the boy's uncle. Why didn't they come back to visit him? Sitting there in the café that night, listening to the rush of talk the colored man made reminded him of the times he would listen to the Italian. He had been so excited and touched to be there with the man that he hardly understood what was being said. And it didn't matter. With his sister and with the Italian he had developed the habit of nodding his head in time to the cadence of people's talk and this was better than listening.

Now he was anxious to test his new sociability. He felt reckless. After all the years of silence, he had talked to the colored boy and to the man in the café; now he wanted to talk to other people. He made a plan: he would go uptown to the store where he bought his provisions and sold his produce. To all the children he passed, he would smile and in this way they would know that there had come a change over him.

Usually, walking through the streets of Beetlecreek, he walked fast, his head bent low as if in anticipation of the stones children sometimes threw at him. Now, however, he walked slowly and boldly in the very middle of the street, his head thrown back and swinging as if inside himself he was singing a song.

All the children were indoors or in school; the streets were deserted. He was very disappointed about this and hurried on to the store.

Up until the moment he entered the store, he didn't know what it was he would buy. Except for the clerk sitting on a barrel reading a newspaper, the store was deserted. "What'll you have?" asked the clerk without looking up. Bill Trapp looked about him. What should he buy? In front of the counter was a high pyramid of Naughton's Toilet Tissues. He pointed to the stack. The clerk seemed astonished and handed him the roll without wrapping it or saying a word. Going out the door, Bill Trapp smiled and called out a squeaking "Good-morning," but the clerk went back to reading the newspaper and didn't return the smile. Outside on the curb, Bill Trapp was so flustered he stumbled and almost fell. He looked around to see if anyone was watching but because of the cold, there were few people on the street.

By the time he was back in Beetlecreek, the colored grade school had let out. Hordes of children ran shrieking up and down the street. He tucked in his belt, straightened his hat and boldly began to walk past them. A determined stiff smile cracked his dry lips. Passing very close to a group of small children—there were three girls and a little boy—he reached out his hand to touch their heads. Up to that moment he may have been unnoticed, but then it seemed as if every child on the block had seen. They became very quiet. It was as if they had all stopped breathing. One of the little girls made a low moan; the other children began to scream.

47

The smallest girl began to cry. They formed a line on either side of him. One boy spit at him. Some of them began yelling hysterically: "Peckerwood, Peckerwood! Ya-aa-a, ya-a-a!" He still smiled stiffly. His hands, still gripping the toilet paper, were dripping sweat. He felt the whizz of a stone pass close to his head and saw the tiny splash it made in a puddle a few yards ahead of him. His steps became faster and faster so that by the time he had passed the last house on the street, he was almost running. Though, walking down the creek road, he felt a danger warning in all that had happened, he refused to let any such thoughts come to his mind. It is all my fault, he kept telling himself. Somehow, what he had done was not right. He was determined not to let himself go back through the tunnel of the years already passed. He was determined to hold on to all he had gained since the day the boy sat on his porch.

Then a strange thing happened. Arriving at his farm, his head bent low, the toilet paper clutched tight as if from it alone could he hope to get relief from the fears that persistently lit up the back of his head, he heard the sound of children laughing. At first he wouldn't look up. Somehow he thought it was some of the children come to follow him. But no! When he looked to see, he saw two little white girls swinging on his gate. Very seldom did white children venture this far down toward the Negro village and he looked upon this scene as a kind of omen. The knowledge that they would know nothing of him gave him courage and once again he tucked in his belt and straightened his hat. He set his lips in a smile and nervously, walking almost sideways, he approached them.

"You all want to go in?" he croaked.

"Why? You live here?" one of the girls asked suspiciously. They were hardly more than eleven years old; both were very blonde with brown eyes. He could tell that they were sisters.

His heart began to beat faster. "Won't you come in?" he asked, his voice shaded in such a way that he might have been making an invitation to a formal dinner party.

Just as he had done the afternoon when Johnny and his uncle were there, he invited the little girls to drink some of the cider. He stuck the battered roll of toilet paper in a drawer and once again looked at himself in the mirror. He

48

was smiling broadly and his yellowed teeth were completely revealed.

He spit into a tin can two yards from the porch and this amused the little girls. One of them tried to spit into the can too, but succeeded only in wetting the front of her coat. This made them all laugh and he spit again to show them how.

Later, he climbed the ladder leaning against one of the apple trees and chose four big apples to give them. Their big brown eyes twinkled to see such fruit and when he saw that it was getting late in the afternoon, he told them that they better be going home. He said this very gently; he didn't want them to get in trouble with their families by coming home late and thus be prevented from coming back the next week to visit him as they had promised.

Already he was so happy he had forgotten completely what had happened while he was on his way back from the store. He walked with the girls to the gate and stood there nibbling at an apple while watching them disappear around the bend in the road.

That night, as a celebration, he drank much dandelion wine. He put on the uniform. He became drunk and took a large quantity of the powder he had used in the Italian's act to burn in the very center of the yard. It made a weird green and red light that silvered up each leaf of the tree and swelled up the pumpkins with a squeezing flicker of shadow. He leaped around through the smoke like a primitive witch doctor, laughing, almost shrieking until he fell exhausted on the steps.

The next morning when he awoke, he was ashamed and took one of the dusty books to look at. He wiped the dust away with an old pair of overalls and sat himself by the window. But reading was impossible; he couldn't keep his eyes away from the road.

Thinking about the little girls, he decided that one of the things he would do, would be to go downtown to the Western Clothing Store to buy a flannel work shirt, maybe a new handkerchief to wear around his neck.

He went to the wall and began raking through the weeds and fallen leaves that grew near the mossy stones. There were vines there that seemed to move and catch themselves to his feet as he walked. Often he put down his rake to look

49

longingly toward the village. He kept hoping that he would see the boy Johnny heading his way.

Finally, he climbed one of the apple trees and spent the rest of the morning like some kind of vulture bird perched on the highest, thinnest limb of the tree, rocked back and forth by the wind, picking his nose in quiet serene anticipation.

■ CHAPTER FOUR

STILL wearing the red, gold, and green fringed apron she had put on to serve Mrs. Pinkerton's Literary Club, Mary ran to the back door to answer the insistent knocking. It was Helen Perkins whose face was blown way up with heavy breathing.

"Mrs. Johnson's dead," she panted, "died this afternoon and Baily Brothers' is doing the arrangements."

The very first thing Mary thought about was of how Mrs. Johnson's death would affect the arrangements for the festival. Would the ladies have to postpone it for another month? she asked herself. They wouldn't, couldn't . . . ! There were still almost ten days left before the festival and ten days, she thought, would be enough time to show respect for the deceased. These calculations she made rapidly in just the time required to coordinate her face muscles into a sorrowful grimace. Secretly she was filled with relief that Mrs. Johnson's death had finally come. For years Mrs. Johnson had been on the point of dying and any real feeling Mary might have summoned had all been spent during the old woman's first strokes.

"Ain't it a pity," Mary said, her voice lowered to a whisper, "she certainly was a wonderful soul. . . ."

For a long time they stood there beside the kitchen table silently reflecting on the old woman's death. "I suppose in the long run it's better," Mary said.

"She certainly was one nice old lady," Helen Perkins said, dabbing at the corners of her eyes with a black handkerchief. They both cried openly, cried as if crying was a bodily function entirely separate from the emotional stimulus. In a few minutes, as if by prearranged signal, they stopped.

"What time you getting off?" Helen Perkins asked.

"Just as soon as I get supper on the table—supposed to get the afternoon off if it wasn't for this here bridge party they had."

The cocoa on the stove began to boil over. "Oh, my Lord," Mary said, giggling like a schoolgirl.

Helen Perkins flopped down in the vacant kitchen chair. "Well, I just thought I'd run over and tell you. Mrs. Ross phoned me and I knew how they are here about you getting calls and all."

"Well, it's mighty nice of you, girl. Glad you came over. You don't suppose they're going to postpone the festival, do you?" Her voice was too anxious. To lessen the effect, she added, " 'Course, they could, it'd be proper and all that, but I was just thinking about them needing the money so bad. . . ."

"Oh, I don't think they would. Funeral most likely be as soon as that girl gets back, ought to be back tonight or latest tomorrow morning."

"I was just asking," Mary said, barely able to conceal her relief. " 'Course, they should have a respectful period. She certainly was a credit to the church. I suppose the Guild will be making a floral offering."

"Mrs. Ross'll be taking care of that like she always does. Unless Mrs. Tolley calls a special meeting about it."

"Well, I'll stop by on my way home and see if there's anything I can do."

But when Mary stopped at the Johnson house on her way home, there was no one there except Mrs. Ross who beckoned her inside the deserted house as if she were welcoming her into the tomb itself. An orange stained rug covered the floor. In the corner by the lamp the rug had been patched up with neat even stitches that unsuccessfully tried to match the pattern of triangles and circles. There was a faint smell of mothballs and furniture polish in the room, and with it, Mary imagined, the tingling animal smell of sickness and death. She glanced toward the ceiling. Mrs. Ross, divining her question, shook her head.

"They been here already. Young Baily hisself come."

They sat on stiff-backed chairs in the living room where later they would put the casket. Mrs. Ross was already dressed in heavy black silk. Mary wondered if she had had the dress already laid out in anticipation of Mrs. Johnson's death. Both of them sat there silently, occasionally moving their heads back and forth as if in answer to questions only they heard.

"I've took up the sheets," Mrs. Ross said. "Put them in the cellar with the rest of the dirty laundry. She certainly was a neat woman, you've got to say that much for her. Those sheets was white as snow."

Mary wanted to leave. She twisted her handkerchief until it was a knot tight as a spring.

Death wasn't real. Death was an occasion for special hymns to be sung, a time when flowers were crowded in a room; death was a time when black was worn—but death wasn't real. There had never been a death in her own immediate family. Once an uncle died and she went with her brothers and sisters to the funeral, had even kissed the corpse. But death was too far away, was too terrible to understand. Death was like looking into a flash of lightning or like looking at the sun without dark glass to look through. Never did it occur to her that she herself would have to die, or if it did occur to her at strange hours of darkness under the covers, she accepted the cold fear that came with it as part of the night, knowing that with the dawn it would have passed.

Besides, Mary didn't live in the present or the past; her life was in the immediate future, and it was the imminent festival that constituted the movement in her life. The festival was the dream she would soon step into, and for this reason, she resented Mrs. Johnson's death.

There was a delicate tapping at the window. An aged woman with yellowish gray eyes and faded clay hands that clutched the air as she walked, entered the room, followed by Helen Perkins. On her head was a fantastic black hat decorated with black gauze flowers. "Howdeedoo, Mrs. Blackburn," they chorused.

Mrs. Blackburn nodded her head and sat herself in the big rocking chair in the corner. She rocked back and forth, occasionally emitting a long, inward sigh. The other two ladies moved their heads back and forth in time with her rocking.

"God always calls home the best of the flock," the old lady croaked in her bubble of a voice.

"Someone's got to stay here tonight, I guess," Mary said, looking down at the floor.

"Well—uh-h . . ." Mrs. Ross began to cough.

"I'll stay," Mrs. Blackburn croaked, "wasn't afraid in life, ain't afraid in death." Her words seemed to swing back and forth from the ceiling.

"I would of stayed myself," Mary said.

"Ain't afraid in life, ain't afraid in death," repeated the old woman.

"If you still got two of them black veils, Mary, can I borrow one of them?" Helen Perkins asked. "I lent mine to Florence."

"The other one ain't so fancy but it's yours if you want it." Mary rose to go. She wanted to talk to her husband, not about the funeral or Mrs. Johnson's death, but about the signs she needed for her booth.

She stood in her doorway watching for him to appear from around the corner. Her breath made a frost pattern on the windowpane. Johnny was upstairs in his room. "Johnny," she called. He didn't answer. She ran to the foot of the steps. The hall light was on but the light was weak and full of holes. "Johnny . . . Johnny . . . what in the world are you doing?"

She was afraid the boy was sick. Ever since the night he had surprised her while she was crying, she had been unable to look him in the face. She wished she had gone to the Principal herself to get special permission for him to begin the school term late. Sometimes she thought of the boy's mother, wondering if she was tall and silent like the son, like her husband. She had never seen any member of their family; the boy was the first and she felt for him the same mixture of awe and ill defined hate she felt for the whole invisible clan standing there behind her husband, watching, measuring anything she did. Still, the boy was poorly and needed looking after. Often he made her think of the child she might have had. Sometimes in the quiet reading of newspapers after supper, she would watch the boy, hoping for a moment when she might say something to him.

He appeared at the top of the steps holding a magazine. His face was immobile, his features elongated in the weak light.

"Oh, there you are," she said; "I just wanted to know where you were and what you were doing."

"I was in my room reading," he said so quietly she could barely make out the words. He turned and went back to his room.

54

She heard the bedsprings creak as he threw his weight across the bed. She stared at the dark space above the stairs feeling alone and a little frightened. She tapped her fingers on the glass and watched people moving past on their way home from work.

■ CHAPTER FIVE

For three days after what happened at the shanty, Johnny wouldn't leave the house. He told his aunt and uncle that he was sick and stayed locked up in his room, throwing himself across the bed every time he heard them coming up the steps. On the table beside his bed was a Bible which from time to time he tried to read, but the strange words printed in finicky type which he couldn't pronounce anyway, all ran together, causing him to give up reading the whole book from the beginning to the end. Many times during the day he would lower the shades and pray, saying, "Most Holy Heavenly Creation of Supreme Benediction, have mercy on my soul. . . ." Sometimes he would just close his eyes and think prayers, bouncing his chin on the mattress or knocking his knees together.

He had little energy and stayed in bed late in the morning with the covers up to his chin. Even while he prayed that God would forgive him for having been with the boys at the shanty, he could see the dirty pictures as plain as day. Then he would place the Bible on his stomach to keep from being tempted.

How ashamed he was of having run away from the shanty! No matter what he told himself about the sinfulness of the boys, he could still hear their mocking laughter. Never again would he be able to face them.

Suddenly, on the third day, he was able to stay in the house no longer, and after lunch when his aunt had gone to Pinkerton's, he jumped out of bed and dressed. He wanted no one to know where he was going so he took a back road.

"Hello, mister," he called.

The old man rushed over to the gate and took hold of Johnny's hand. He was breathing hard and Johnny could feel the coarse imprint of a wart as the man's blunt fingers closed over his own.

"So you did come back, boy," the old man said, breathing hard through his nose right into Johnny's face.

Johnny tried to smile. The man had thrust his face close to Johnny's as if to see him better and once Johnny saw the reflection of his own face in the man's pearl-liquid eyes. "I was just passing by and I thought I'd drop in," Johnny said.

"Oh, I'm glad you did, glad you did, boy."

Maybe he shouldn't have come, Johnny thought. What if the man was crazy like they said he was. He certainly acted nervous and shaky.

"Well, let's not us stand right here in the middle of the yard like this, huh, Johnny. That's the name, ain't it? Johnny. I don't forget no names much." He laughed then, a low squashed laugh that seemed to be put into him by a ventriloquist.

The laugh made Johnny uneasy.

"You tell your uncle I'm much obliged he took me to the café that night. Yessir, a man gets lonely all by hisself out here. I tell you, boy. I could tell you a thing or two about being alone out here. Yessir. . . ."

Johnny saw the old man looking under a bush. He too began looking there.

"See there under that bush?" Bill Trapp said. "There's an old granddaddy garter snake under there about a yard long. I just been waiting here for the bugger to come on out. It's got a nest under there, I reckon."

Johnny looked under the bush where the man pointed. He wasn't exactly afraid of snakes because he had learned in nature study class that garter snakes weren't poisonous, but the idea of a snake, long, slimy, and green-embossed there in the yard with Bill Trapp unnerved him. For a long time they stood there waiting, neither speaking. Johnny stole a look at the man and saw that his mouth was set in a pleasant smile and that the flesh of his jaws swung from the smile like taffy in a taffy machine. Once the old man caught Johnny's eyes and Johnny flushed.

Johnny could no longer remember what his father looked like. He had only a hazy vision of a kind smile. What he did remember, however, was the feeling of his father's face. Long after his father died, he remembered that feeling. Sometimes he would see pictures of men in magazines that could recall that feeling; these pictures, he would carefully tear out and paste into a scrapbook. But even walking on the streets, he would sometimes exchange glances with men and experience for a moment the feeling of his father's face. It had to do with the way the head was held and the light that came from the eyes. Looking at the old white man, Johnny realized for the first time that there was this feeling about him.

They went to the porch and the old man brought out the bottle of cider and glasses. For a long time they sat drinking without saying a word. Johnny tried and tried to think of something to say but he couldn't. Still, sitting there with the white man, he felt comfortable, as if he belonged. After all, he thought, the old man was just like Mr. Lewis, the janitor at school, or Mr. Miller, the fireman, or like any of the white people he had grown up with on his street in Pittsburgh. He didn't have to pretend with them. He could tell what they were thinking and not have to try to figure out what they really meant when they said something. He felt closer to the old white man than he did to his Uncle David even.

"We're friends, ain't we, boy?" the old man asked suddenly.

Johnny smiled and held out his hand. It made him feel gracious to do such a thing; it was a gallant gesture, he thought, and it made him feel better already. He could feel the wart again.

"Well, I didn't know. I thought you'd be mad and all because I chased the boys and . . ."

"Ah, them. They're just a bunch of rowdies," Johnny said quickly. "I don't hang around with them regular."

"I never would of chased them only they never come and asked like decent people should."

After a while, Bill Trapp told Johnny about when he was with the carnival and Johnny felt quite like a man listening to the stories Bill Trapp told. He liked best the stories about the Italian trapeze artist and the stuffed dog, and the story about a time when a storm blew down the big tent and the wild beasts ran through the crowd causing panic. These stories evoked new worlds for Johnny, worlds far from Beetlecreek and he was sorry when the old man stopped to go look at the traps.

It was as they were walking from the edge of the wood, back to the house through the uncut weeds along the stone-wall, through the goldenrod and faded thistle, that they saw the two little Negro girls standing outside the gate peeping in.

Both were dressed identically in long tweed coats that reached to their ankles. From out on the road where they stood, the two little girls couldn't see Johnny and Bill Trapp.

One of them, apparently the oldest, was saying, "Come on now, what're you waiting for—you scared?"

With the little girls was a long yellow puppy that ran back and forth between the girls, whining.

The old man nudged Johnny and called to the two little girls. "Hello, there, Miss Prissies! What you all doing out there? If you got a notion to come in, why don't you come in instead of standing out there with your teeth in your mouth."

And at the sound of the old man's voice, the little girls jumped back. The smallest girl stood behind the oldest who extended her arms as if to shield and protect the other. Both of them were very young, probably no more than eight years old, Johnny thought. Their eyes were shiny with fear, and their mouths open.

Finally, the younger of them broke into a smile—a full-toothed happy smile that made even Johnny smile. And when the older girl saw the old man and Johnny smile, she lowered her shielding arms.

"Good morning, sir," she said. "My mother told me to ask you for some pumpkins. . . ." "It's for a benefit," added the smaller girl.

"Oh, ho! It's pumpkins you want, is it?" Bill Trapp said. "Well now, the first thing you better do is come inside the gate, else you won't get nothing."

And Johnny, still smiling because the two little girls were lovely with their pigtails and their tiny-tooth smiles, opened the gate for them and they marched solemnly inside the yard.

"What's your names? . . . Mary Ellen and Sarah Tolley, huh? Well, well, well! They sure is right smart names." Bill Trapp's voice was low-pitched and very kind. "Come on up here to the porch and sit down a spell," he commanded.

Soon, they were relaxed on the warm steps in the sunshine and the dog came to lie at their feet, his eyes half closed, his tongue sleeping on his teeth.

"What will you do with the pumpkins?" Bill Trapp asked them.

"Well, sir," began Mary Ellen, the older of the two, "we'll cut faces in them and Mom'll use them to dec'rate the booths with at the festival. It's a *benefit*, you see." And she pronounced the word very carefully.

Sarah, the youngest, said, "Mom's the president of the Guild. . . ."

After a while, Bill Trapp asked them if they wouldn't like to have some fresh apple cider.

"Oh my, yes indeed," said Sarah.

"Why, thank *you*, mister, it will certainly be a treat."

While the old man was inside rinsing out the glasses, Sarah said to Johnny, "He sure is a nice white man, isn't he? I sure was scared to come out here, but Mom said wasn't nothin to be afraid of any more. . . ."

And Mary Ellen, who was looking around the yard at the fruit trees, and especially the shiny pumpkins, nodded her head emphatically, "Hm-m,m-mm! He sure is!"

Johnny just smiled. He was glad the old man was being so kind to the little girls.

Then Bill Trapp brought them glasses filled to the brim with fizzling cider, and after a while, the sun moved and their shadows stretched behind them toward the doorway. In the yard, the shadows under the trees were like jigsaw puzzles suddenly broken.

"Well, now, I think we better go and see about getting you straightened out about the pumpkins," Bill Trapp said, stretching his arms high above him and far behind him like a man doing morning exercises. And the four of them—now they were very gay—went to the yard where the pumpkins were.

The yellow puppy dog rose from its sleep and stretched too, and he trailed along behind them. Sarah danced lightly between the rows of the pumpkins.

"Gal, you be careful what you doin!" said Mary Ellen, trying hard to be proper. But she had to laugh. And so did Bill Trapp, only his laugh was deep and vibrating while the girl's was a fragile, porcelain laugh.

"Now then," said Bill Trapp pompously, "we'll have to pick us out the biggest and bestest pumpkins here for jack o'lantern making. Look sharp now!"

After they had carefully considered all the pumpkins in the garden, some of which were long, and others of which were fat and round with wet, light yellowish spots on them, they decided on three gigantic ones, thoroughly ripe and almost red in color.

Bill Trapp took his penknife and skillfully separated them from their stalks. Johnny had to help him cut through the tough fiber.

Mary Ellen tried to lift her pumpkin but it was so large, she had to hold it in the cradle of her arms. Sarah kneeled beside hers and caressed it, letting her fingers slip lovingly from edge to ridge.

"Why, I think them pumpkins is going to be too heavy for you kids to carry." He scratched his chin with his big red fingers as if struggling with a perplexing problem.

"Oh, no sir!" said Mary Ellen anxiously, "we can carry them all right." And then, as if to prove it, she hugged the pumpkin close to her and began walking away.

Sarah almost dropped hers with the effort, but managed to stagger a few steps further before Bill Trapp stopped her.

"Hold on, now! Ain't no need of all that hard work," he said. "Put them pumpkins down."

And when the girls turned to look at him, pleading with their eyes, he added, "I'll get my wheelbarrow and we'll load her up to the top with all the pumpkins we can carry—now how about that?"

Johnny could have danced for happiness and relief. At first, the girls couldn't speak but when he brushed past them to fetch the wheelbarrow, they murmured thanks. As soon as he was out of sight, they put their arms around each other and danced. Then they ran around the garden, getting in each other's way in a happy, frantic search for more, even larger pumpkins.

Their shrieks of delight excited the dog and he jumped up and down all around them and licked the pumpkins and made water on a pile of leaves near the fence. Then Bill Trapp returned, wheeling the wheelbarrow in front of him, turning to this side and that, pretending that he didn't know how to manage it. This made the girls almost double up with laughter.

They loaded the wheelbarrow until not another pumpkin would fit.

WILLIAM DEMBY

"Gee, mister," Sarah exclaimed, "our mom's sure going to be thankful for these pumpkins."

"Yessirree!" echoed Mary Ellen, "with these jack-lanterns we goin have *some* benefit."

Johnny walked alongside of the wheelbarrow to help hold on the pile of pumpkins. The little girls, as if frightened that the pumpkins would disappear, walked on either side of the wheelbarrow, each resting one hand on the pile.

The sun was hot on the road and the wheelbarrow made a squeaking sound as it rolled unsteadily along.

When they were almost to the village and while the two little girls were running ahead to chase the puppy, Bill Trapp told Johnny:

"I think these little girls is about the nicest children I ever been around. I ain't never had no children of my own. I was adopted. I used to live in a orphanage. 'Course that's way long ago, Johnny."

Johnny was embarrassed. While he was trying to think of something to say, the old man stopped the wheelbarrow.

"You know what, boy? I'm going to have a picnic for these little girls, a little get together. Yessir, boy. And there's some other kids. Kids from Ridgeville. I'm going to have a picnic and let 'em play in the yard. What do you think of that, Johnny?"

The old man seemed so excited, that Johnny became nervous. He had been thinking of what a strange sight the four of them must be: the old white man, the two little girls holding hands and marching ahead, the ancient wheelbarrow loaded high with pumpkins—

"Why, I could turn the place into a regular playground."

Johnny started to walk on. "I think that might be a fine idea," he said, but he wasn't really listening. As he turned the corner, he saw a crowd gathered around a long, black hearse, shiny and low-slung like a super, enameled beetle, too elegant and foreign looking for the shabby street, parked in front of the Johnson house.

She's dead, he thought with horror.

By that time, they were approaching the edge of the crowd. Johnny saw old women in the crowd. He saw old Mrs. Johns running her fingers over the black, shiny metal of the fender. But most of the old people were on porches, looking toward the crowd, toward the hearse, elemental fear in their

62

eyes as if, Johnny imagined, they were afraid there had been some mistake and the undertaker had come for them.

A small boy, his trousers half falling off him, ran up and down the street pulling a skate wheel wagon behind him. This was the only sound, the midget clanging of skate wheels on brick, the only sound, for there was the heavy silence of respect for death.

Mary Ellen and Sarah were excited. "It's Baily Brothers' hearse!" they exclaimed, "Baily Brothers'!"

Johnny saw the Leader and Baby Boy standing on the inside of the crowd close to the hearse so he wouldn't push his way closer. Instead he stood on tiptoes on the curb and watched what was going on.

Two pale-faced white men jumped from the cab and came around to the back of the hearse to get the stretchers. One of them, a serious eyed young man, seemed embarrassed by the crowd that pressed so close to the vehicle. All around him were the sullen, awe-struck faces that evaluated his every move. Once he caught Johnny's eye and Johnny looked away, ashamed.

One of the men from the undertakers was dressed in a gray business suit. His manner had the gentle efficiency of a woman and when he wasn't moving, he flicked his fingernails clean with his thumbnail.

"That's Mr. Baily, himself," someone whispered to Johnny.

"All right, all right, let's not crowd around here," Mr. Baily said. And his voice was sweet and high as a woman's.

While the undertakers were inside, people talked softly and uneasily among themselves, glancing from time to time up to Mrs. Johnson's window. There was one old lady standing near Johnny who kept repeating under her breath, "When yo time comes and He takes yo to His bosom, yo must rise and follow . . . yo must rise and follow. . . ."

Johnny could see the white tufts of hair on the back of the woman's neck, and he was filled with loathing for her.

In a short while, the door of the house opened and the two men from the undertakers appeared with the stretcher. There was a long lump under the white canvas; a long sigh from the crowds. Then silence.

And after the hearse had pulled away and there was still smoke from the exhaust, the people wouldn't leave, but stood unsatisfied, as if in a stupor, silent and glum, staring toward the corner where the hearse had disappeared.

Johnny forgot about the pumpkins and the old man until one of the girls pulled on his sleeve. "Ain't you going to help take the pumpkins home no more?"

Johnny could feel the people focusing their attention on him and the old man. He was slightly ashamed although he didn't know why. He tried to walk ahead but his legs moved stiffly as they would in a dream. He wanted to say something to Bill Trapp so that it would look natural his being with him, but he could think of nothing to say. The old man kept his eyes on the pumpkins, looking neither right nor left, cutting with the wheelbarrow the stares that fenced them in.

Mrs. Tolley was standing on the porch waiting for them when they arrived. "I saw you all comin from way down the street. Lord, look at them pumpkins!" She came waddling to the fence, walking with her eyes staring fixedly at the pumpkins.

She looks like she could have been the barber's sister, Johnny thought.

Both the little girls began talking at once. Bill Trapp, smiling, stood beside the wheelbarrow, obviously embarrassed by the commotion. Johnny pretended to straighten the pumpkins, but he was anxious to get away.

The street was full of bird excitement and sunset excitement, and the people who had seen dead Mrs. Johnson were loath to leave the street so that there was movement back and forth and across. Some of them looked in at the pumpkins and Bill Trapp.

Mrs. Tolley lifted one of the pumpkins, hugging it close to her pendulous breasts, weighing it with her hands.

"All I can say," she said, addressing the people looking in from the sidewalk, "is that it's surely nice of him to give the church these pumpkins, and we won't forget it."

When all the pumpkins were loaded on the porch and there was nothing more to say and Johnny and Bill Trapp and the little girls all stood waiting for something, Mrs. Tolley smiled her church smile again and said, rather formally, "Mr. Trapp, I want you to know we're thankful to you for your kindness and won't you come in and have a cup of chocolate?"

But Bill Trapp refused, saying he really must be going, that he had work to do. Awkwardly, he said good-bye to the girls, and they curtsied to him, and their mother smiled, and Johnny shook hands with Bill Trapp, and all of them watched him push his wheelbarrow down the street toward the creek road.

Now there was the slanted light of sunset that made the street brilliant copper, and swarms of birds swooped screeching on every perch, restless, unsatisfied, tearing apart the space between roof and sky. It was a melancholy fall sight and it made Johnny very sad. And Black Enameled Death that he had seen represented everything of Beetlecreek and was like the restlessness and dissatisfaction of the birds only inside him, swarming and swooping inside him, filling him with vague fear and shame, preparing him for something, telling him, warning him, separating him from things that were happening around him, apart from him, pulling him along toward things he could not see or know.

He was relieved to see the yellow puppy dog that had been with them that afternoon and he chased it. And when he caught it, he held it close to him, close to his head so that the warm licking sound filled his ears and shut out the evening screams of the birds.

PART THREE

■ CHAPTER ONE

WHEN Edith Johnson entered Telrico's that night, everyone stopped talking to turn around and watch. The way she walked was big city—slowly, dragging the hind foot a little, swinging the hips gently, holding onto her purse with both hands. Her head was held high, but not so high she didn't make everyone feel she was looking right at them. She was dressed big city, too; she wore a black suit, the narrow skirt of which wasn't tight or short enough to be called cheap. But it was short and tight enough. She wasn't brown colored or yellow colored. Edith Johnson's skin was gray— the way they look in nightclubs. And her hair was brushed straight down on the sides, glistening black cat hair. Her eyes were the color of a rotogravure newspaper and her lips were newly painted red.

She slipped onto a stool and whispered something to Telrico, who immediately shuffled away to the cooler and brought back a bottle of beer, carefully wiping it off before setting it down in front of her.

There she is. Edith Johnson is back! No one said it, but the words were there in the first quiet of her entrance. For a moment no one moved; each waited for the other. Then, suddenly, there was a general movement in her direction.

"Hello there, gal!" "Well, look who's back!" "Honey chile. . . ." "How's the big city gal?" "You sure is lookin good!"

They wiped their hands before shaking hands with her and they looked at her black suit of mourning.

David had turned with the rest of them to watch her come in. He was sitting alone in the only vacant booth.

There she is, after all these years, there she is. He almost spoke the words aloud, so great was his agitation. She has changed very much—lost that little girl look. But then she'd begun losing that look the last time he saw her at college.

He turned his back to her and began tearing the wet labels from the empty beer bottles in front of him, rolling them into a ball and chewing them. He had put on his Sunday suit, but now he was glad he didn't wear a tie. It would have been too obvious. As it was his wife asked him what the occasion was.

After all these years, she was back, and he wondered if she even remembered him.

Seemingly, hours went by, and he became deaf to the noise of the café.

"You don't mind if I sit down, do you . . . David?"

It was her voice! He turned, and there she was smiling down on him, holding her hand out for him to shake. Her voice was huskier than he remembered it, but eight years had gone by.

Too quickly and roughly he took her hand. He was ashamed that his fingers were sweating so.

"God, no. Sit down, stranger!" He had started to rise, but thought better of it before he was half out of his seat.

"More beer," she called to Telrico. Then she pulled a cigarette out of her pocketbook and sat with her eyebrows raised waiting for a light.

"Oh, Jesus, excuse me," David said, fumbling clumsily for a match. He was too nervous. He looked at her closely while he lit the cigarette.

Her face was fatter and there were fern-like wrinkles under her eyes, but the lips were nervous and always slightly parted just as he remembered.

"I'm sorry about your mother," he said.

She didn't answer him but sat with her eyebrows raised, smiling across the table at him. It was the same smile that used to make him think she was laughing at him.

He didn't know what to say after that. She wouldn't answer him. He thought she was acting very strangely. He was still surprised that she had come to speak to him and drink with him.

After a while she said, "It sure makes you feel funny coming back after being away for such a long time. Everything is changed . . . or maybe it's that there ain't nothing changed . . . it's all so scary. . . ."

70

There was something frightening in the way she cowered in the corner of the booth, the way her body hunched forward as if it were an unbearable weight to her. He wondered if it were only his imagination.

"It has been a long time," he said.

"Just about eight years . . . and you married Mary."

"And you went to the city. . . ."

". . . and didn't marry anybody," she said, laughing.

The top button of her jacket was unbuttoned. He remembered how at college he would sit in his room and watch her pass on the walk below, surrounded by many boys who knew how to keep her excited and interested, boys who knew what she wanted.

"How old are you?" she asked. She filled their glasses and licked the foam from her fingers.

He hesitated a moment before answering; he had almost forgotten his age. "Going on thirty-two."

"And I'm going on twenty-seven. You used to be one serious boy. Everybody thought you was going to be something."

He laughed and laughed, partly from shame, partly from anger, partly to relieve the tension. He laughed so loudly, that people turned around to look at him.

Wilson came over to the booth and sat down beside Edith. He nodded casually to David and pressed himself close to the girl.

"Well, sugar lump, how is you?"

He was smoking a large cigar and his hat was pushed way back off his forehead. There was a little mirror against the wall, part of a beer advertisement, that he looked into to check his appearance. He was dressed in a black silk shirt and wore a white tie that hung down below the line of his belt. He was all mouth smiling down on her. With his free hand he groped clumsily for her shoulder. Wilson was forty years old and unmarried, but he affected the manner and dress of the adolescents.

"Hello," Edith said calmly.

David wondered why she didn't make some move to get away from Wilson's embrace. It made him angry to see her relax in his arms.

"I suah is sorry about your mother, honeychile," Wilson said. "She was one sweet person, but we all knows that

71

when yo time comes, there ain't nothin to do but go."

David wanted to laugh. How funny for Wilson to be expressing such sentiments. He wondered why the girl didn't laugh.

Wilson finally left them and once again, they were alone. Edith filled his glass from a small whiskey bottle she had in her purse. "Brought it all the way from Pittsburgh," she said proudly. Mixed with the beer, it left a strange, gluey taste in his mouth.

Once she said (she was getting a little drunk, he thought), "You remember the time you took me to the dance at State and told me you loved me? You were cute."

She brushed her knee against his under the table and allowed it to remain.

David wanted to say something but he was all choked. He couldn't tell whether it was the whiskey or his excitement that caused his wrists to shake so.

"Bring me another beer, Sam," she called to Telrico. "Don't worry," she said to David when she caught his eye, "I've got money to pay for it."

A flash of anger passed over him. He wondered if she were mocking him.

When she opened her pocketbook, she took out a black lace handkerchief with which to wipe her face. Only then, seeing her fingers crumble the brittle lace scrollwork, did he realize completely Mrs. Johnson's death.

How could the girl be in the café drinking when her mother was dead in the parlor!

Then he became afraid of the girl as he used to be afraid of her. He realized anew the strength of her, the defiance of her. Now he understood how it was that the girl could leave the sick mother alone; and the knowledge excited him. He imagined he could feel the strength of her evil coursing through the knee contact, imagined he felt the electric sensation of her.

"It's so damn funny to be here," she said. "Nothing really changed. All the same people living their lives in somebody's kitchen or hotel lobby."

She ran her hand through her hair and blew smoke from her nostrils.

He thought she was talking too loudly and stole a look

around the room to see if anyone was watching him. But, by now, Telrico's was all noise, smoke, and drunken gaiety.

"Mrs. Johnson, she thought she was giving me everything I wanted but the only thing I ever wanted was to get away from her and this rotten town. I didn't ask her to bring me here, I wasn't none of hers. She didn't care a damn about me except to show everybody what a good Christian she was and to get money from the county. She used to keep me from enjoying anything unless she was the one that invented it. She and her stinking church organizations. . . ."

Later she asked him, "What're you so quiet about? You sure are serious. You're the only one in this town ever knew what a coffin this town was and you from upstate. Why didn't you leave?"

He was afraid now. He filled his glass, swallowed it, and got up out of his seat as if to go. The mixture of beer and whiskey had gone to his head and he wanted to get away from the girl.

"You ain't going to leave me here all by myself, are you?" she asked with mock distress.

"I've . . . I've got to get up in the morning early," he stammered.

"How about walking me home?" she asked coyly, catching onto the tail of his coat, running her tongue over her top lip, holding his glance.

They didn't say a word to each other until they came to the creek road. She walked very close to him, occasionally bumping her hip against his. The sound from Telrico's became thinner and thinner until it was drowned out by the sound of their own footsteps and the sound of the creek.

"Now that you're all alone in the world," he asked her, "what'll you do?"

"Nothing. I've always been alone. Go back to the city."

"If you don't mind my asking, what do you do there? You got a job?"

She laughed and laughed. They were crossing the swinging bridge and, underneath them, the creek scratched the reeds. The Streamliner roared alongside the hills and screamed past the station without slowing down until it came to Munstor. The swinging bridge swung grandly back and forth, side to side.

"Do you feel bad because she's dead?" He was sorry as

73

soon as he asked her. He knew exactly what she would say. He held his breath waiting.

At first she didn't answer. He couldn't see her face, but he knew her face was lowered.

"I hated her," she said, finally.

As soon as they had crossed the bridge and were walking alongside the creek in a place shielded from the moonlight by a row of bushes, she stopped and pulled his head down to hers.

He was unable to breathe. The openings of his nostrils seemed too small and his mouth squashed hers.

"I didn't expect that," he said, as soon as he caught his breath.

"It wasn't all that bad, was it?"

"I don't reckon so. . . ."

He wanted to laugh, to shout, to run.

"What're you laughing at?" she asked.

"Everything! Just everything!"

"You sure are funny. . . ."

And while she kissed his ears, he thought of all those Sunday afternoons, alone in his room with his fantasies and the books, and of the sound of her laughing on the steps of the girls' dormitory. And all the while, he could see that bare room. . . .

The light was on in the bedroom. His wife was under the covers looking up at the ceiling. She didn't turn her head when he entered.

"What time is it?" she asked.

"I don't know, must be a little after eleven o'clock." He hoped she wasn't going to make a scene. He was too excited, too happy. . . .

"Mrs. Pinkerton's giving me off for the funeral—you're going too, aren't you?"

My God! He had forgotten the funeral. He sat on the bed and began taking off his shoes. As if for the first time, he saw how run-down at the heels they were. He must get them repaired or, better yet, get new ones. He went to the bathroom and looked at himself in the mirror. Have I changed much, he wondered. The funeral tomorrow—he'd have to go; she would be there.

"What time is it—the funeral?" he asked her.

"Well, I got to get to the church early, about nine-thirty, but it don't start until ten."

He went back to the bathroom to wash his teeth, lingering a long time before the mirror to examine himself. He decided that his teeth were getting bad and that his hair was getting thin. He rubbed his cheeks vigorously to bring color to them, but in the harsh greenish light, the flesh seemed even more greasy and unhealthy. He remembered how he used to get up early in the morning to run around the campus to keep himself in trim. Strange to see how age gets hold of the flesh.

She was still awake when he came back to the room.

"That Edith Johnson's back, ain't she? Leastways, Helen Perkins said she come back."

He sat on the side of the bed with his back toward her. His heart was pounding. "Yeah, she's back. I saw her in Telrico's."

"That's one rotten girl, her mother laid out dead and she galavantin around beer gardens."

David cringed. He snapped off the light, then rolled into bed, lying on the very edge on his side so he could drag his hand on the floor.

"You used to be sweet on her, didn't you?" she said, laughing a low-breathed laugh. "Never would give you a tumble though, would she? But you just go up there to the city and see her on the streets. . . ."

Rage swelled up within, but he controlled his breathing so she couldn't feel his anger.

Of course the girl had changed, he thought, yet there was about her all that he had liked before: the smile that no longer immobilized him, the loose way she had of standing with her hips off balance, and the way she had of staring straight into his eyes with her lips slightly parted. But most of all he liked the daredevil in her.

His wife was asleep. He could hear her heavy, asthmatic breathing. Without looking, he knew she lay, as always, with her head turned to one side, her mouth open and gasping for air, one arm stretched back of her toward the wall.

The beer and whiskey began to wear off and his head ached. One day several years before, he was sitting on the porch with his wife, when the ice cream man passed He bought two ice cream sticks and while he was carrying them

WILLIAM DEMBY

back, he dropped one of them. His wife cried and cried and there was nothing he could do to console her. He thought of the day he bought a new slip for his wife; she accepted the gift without thanking him, but continued wearing the torn, gray stained one for weeks after. Edith's things were big-city silk. He tried not to think of what he had done with the girl. Tomorrow would be the funeral and he would have to go. He would have to look at the dead mother and the daughter, knowing how the girl had talked about the mother, realizing that all knew how he felt about the girl. He remembered how quiet Telrico's became that night he entered holding onto Bill Trapp's arm—how they moved aside and stared. And he remembered how, all the time they were in there, Telrico's stayed subdued and quiet.

But maybe that was the reason for bringing Bill Trapp to the village, to prove to them that the old man wasn't the strange, mysterious inhabitant of the old May Farm.

Or maybe, and he decided this was the most likely, he just liked to talk to the old man. There was in the old man, the quality of listening and understanding that he hadn't found in anyone before. In their talk that first afternoon, when he had gone to get Johnny, he had discovered that the old man understood what he thought, could help him interpret for himself the jumble of ideas he had accumulated during all these years.

Then too, he could tell that the old man was lonely. And this moved him. This, at least, he could understand.

Maybe, now, things would be different with Bill Trapp. They were saying at the barbershop that the old man must be all right to make a donation like that to the church.

After the funeral, he would go to visit the old man and tell him what people were saying about the pumpkins.

76

■ CHAPTER TWO

THE funeral was over and David stood with his back to the gay whispering. They still hadn't brought the casket out and people had already lined the walk waiting for the procession. Mary had wanted him to volunteer as a pallbearer but he had refused, saying that his dark suit was too raggedy. But that had been only partly true. The real reason, he knew, was that he was afraid to come too close to the coffin. Once his mother had made him kiss a dying aunt who suffered from a disease that prevented her from being washed. And it was that smell he smelled in the church.

He puffed and puffed on the cigarette, blowing great clouds of smoke. Three white taxi drivers were sitting on the curbstone beside their cabs, waiting for the people to come out. Baily Brothers' hearse was there surrounded by a group of admiring children.

Over the hill, beyond the curve of the creek, it was already raining, but over the church, the sky was clear gray.

He had entered the church late and had had to sit in the front row where the seats made an arc around the altar. For a long time he kept his eyes to the floor refusing to look at anyone, imagining all the while that they watched him, watched him to see if he would look at the girl seated just off the center aisle in the front row.

During a long prayer, while the congregation stood with bowed heads, he looked at her. For just a moment she returned his look, and then she winked. Immediately he turned to look at his wife to see if she had seen, but her eyes were closed tight—she was listening to the prayer. When, with the rest of the congregation, he filed past the coffin to have a last look at the remains, Edith kicked him gently.

They brought the coffin out and shoved it into Baily

77

Brothers' hearse. David stood aside and turned his head so that he wouldn't have to look at her as she walked behind the short procession. Once he was tempted to turn around to see if she were crying, but he knew she would be walking just as she walked the first time she came in Telrico's, aloof, graceful, disdainful of the whole show.

Just when he was about to walk away, his wife caught up to him. She carried her choir robes folded on her arm.

"What's the matter you not going to the cemetery?"

"I've got a headache," he explained.

"You better spend some of that money you drink up at Telrico's to go downtown and see Dr. Epstein, else you ain't going to be long with this world."

But he knew she thought he was lying.

Sitting in the corner against the white wall of the church, he thought of being trapped in the village, arrested, closed in.

Often he would sit on the railing of the swinging bridge, looking down at the creek, watching the current. He would watch floating things—boxes, tin cans, bottles. He would watch how some of these things became trapped in the reeds alongside the shore. First there was a whirlpool to entice the floating object, then a slow-flowing pool, and finally, the deadly mud backwater in the reeds. In the reeds would be other objects already trapped.

This was Beetlecreek, he thought. And he knew that, like the rusty cans, he was trapped, caught, unable to move again.

This was like when he first became aware of being suffocated—the suffocation he had felt in church, the undercurrent of secret excitement he knew they felt partaking of the death ritual, the secret envy for the escape death offered, the jealousy of the escaped one; the hunger to be joined together in something, anything, even the celebration of death; the secret meanings communicated seated before the corpse; the feast; the singing; the sermon; the joviality of the handshakes on the porch steps; the admiration of Baily Brothers' shiny new hearse; the terrible importance of Death to lives that had little importance; the justification of life in death. He too had felt all these things, knowing at the same time that his feeling for the girl had meaning only because it brought movement to his life (a life which had become static, caught in the creek reeds, turned rusty and muddy),

78

had importance because it lifted the suffocation from him.

The minor pitched service had increased in pace. The atmosphere seemed to become more and more intense as with the common intake of breath. (He thought, It is all one big lung, one single felt fear. . . .) Then it was that his thoughts became clear, like standing on top of a mountain and he could see way back through the years, way back through the years to a time that might have been the beginning of what he was feeling now.

Because one day the grade school teachers took him to a museum and showed him the pictures. It was the first time he had ever seen anything like it. It made him feel funny, like as if he needed something he couldn't put his finger on, like he never felt before it made him feel. And ever after that time, he looked at all the pictures he could. Then he began drawing pictures himself. At first, when his father saw what he was doing, he didn't say anything; but later, when he began to take drawing lessons at school, his father said he was wasting his time and that he should be taking the commercial course to prepare himself for a white collar job. So he stopped the drawing lessons. Instead, he began to print signs and this his father liked because he often earned spending money. But there was no getting away from the strange feeling of being unsatisfied, which was a true strange feeling which often kept him from eating. Especially when he looked at pictures. Sometimes he would want to cry because it wasn't he who had painted the picture.

He would walk five miles to the county library to get books that had reproductions in them. Reading kept him from feeling as if he were tied up in a knot. For a little while he could forget that he was a Negro. When he was very young, there was no need for it. Up there in Pittsburgh it was being a kid first and it didn't make any difference that he was a Negro. But when he went to that Negro college, he began to feel it, and along with it, the feeling of being suffocated and unable to move. This had nothing to do with his not having opportunities or "civil rights," but it was a strange feeling, very difficult for him to explain to himself, which had to do with feeling Death, feeling frozen, suffocated, unable to breathe, knowing there was little to be done about it.

And looking at pictures or reading books, he didn't have that feeling.

And that first year at college, he had tried to investigate all the ways there were of getting away from the death-grip feeling. So he read books, looked at pictures, and began listening to music. But in this, he was all alone because, he soon discovered, no one else at that college wanted really to escape from the death-grip feeling, even though, he knew, all of them felt it in one way or another. They were satisfied or resigned and had learned how to get pleasure from it instead of from the things which could help them escape from it.

And it wasn't long before he discovered what these other means of escape were, and he learned about goodtiming with girls and drinking. This was the easiest way, and you could goodtime yourself out of being suffocated.

But this wasn't at all like looking at pictures and reading books and he was afraid and unsatisfied; suddenly he realized that he was getting used to the goodtiming. More and more difficult was it becoming to find the real secret of escape. And of this, he was afraid, but he had no strength to change. The easy way kept coming back to him with ever increasing strength until there was no more looking at pictures, no more reading books, no more listening to music, only the goodtimes and the easy way to escape the feeling of the death-grip.

But sometimes, like a quick glimpse of light behind flapping curtains, it would come back. And this would be such a time as walking across the campus early in the morning when there was still mist and maybe only a lonely pigeon walking on the road. Then the meaning of it all would be clear to him. Maybe only a color or a sound would prod him, but he would know then that the way he was doing it was all wrong, and he would become sad and dissatisfied and ashamed. Times like those, he could separate himself from being Negro, times like that, he would be one size bigger than man.

But then, as soon as he saw one person, as soon as he heard one person speak, the vision would disappear, and being in the death-grip would seem the most natural and permanent thing in the world.

Then he would go back to goodtiming, all the while feeling

himself getting deeper and deeper and the death-grip becoming stronger and stronger. More and more he became a kind of clown and less and less he was a man, and more and more he was like the rest of them, and all together they goodtimed their way into forgetting the death-grip.

Then, one summer, he came to Beetlecreek.

Edith Johnson was in college with him, and he loved her secretly and weakly, and pinned all kinds of fancy dreams on her. She became the symbol of his escape from the goodtime world (which was a funny thing since she was one of the leaders of the goodtime set on the campus), but he did, and for that reason, he could never summon enough courage to talk to her. Others told her that he was crazy about her and she didn't mind, but she would hardly look at him and kept herself busy with the goodtime crowd.

Once he took her to a dance. Her current boy friend was one of his roommates. Just before the dance, the roommate passed out from too much cheap gin and wine, so he dressed himself up in the roommate's tuxedo and carnation and took her to the dance. The only chance he had to speak to her (he had had only one dance with her and was hardly able to breathe) was on the way home. Somehow he managed to flood out to her the story of the death-grip and how he needed her to make his escape.

She laughed and laughed as if it were the funniest thing in the world and the next day, the whole campus laughed and laughed, and his roommates laughed and laughed, and the rest of that year was miserable for him. So he resolved to goodtime better and harder than any of the rest of them, only he had little money to spend and had to work.

That summer, he came to Beetlecreek with the excuse of visiting a friend, a classmate of his, but the real reason was to see the girl. But again he was so shy that he never spoke to her. Some mornings, he would rise very early just so he could watch her come out on her back porch to sew. Other times he would walk way out of his way to see her cross the swinging bridge.

But then there was another girl, older than this one, named Mary Philips, who had never been away from Beetlecreek. This girl said she wanted to meet the boy from Pittsburgh and State College.

He met her and the second time they were together, they

went to the church grass. So well had he learned how to act by then, so well had he learned the easy ways to escape the death-grip, so well, that he was able to convince himself that he loved her. And he may have, because in those days she was not a maid, and not bitter, but was a happy girl full of the natural prettiness of the young, graceful with a cute way of swinging her body when she walked, always wearing nice, blowy blouses. He loved her, he thought, and went with her many times to the church grass. Before he knew it, he had forgotten all about the death-grip, had forgotten all about Edith.

Forgetting Edith was like getting out of prison. For the first time in a long while, he was able to feel himself as belonging entirely to himself. And during that summer, it was a wonderful feeling. He had a girl and she wanted him. It was like a ceremony on becoming a man, a line dividing boy and man, but more than that, he thought, a line dividing life and death. And he wondered why he ever needed the books and the music. For the first time in all those years, he was really a free man.

When he went back to college that fall, everyone noticed the change in him and respected him for it.

One day, she wrote him a letter on tablet paper saying that she was going to have a baby. That was the end for him.

He came to Beetlecreek and did his duty, and later, he realized that to be trapped was inevitable and that all his life had been heading in that direction. Marrying the girl was like jumping over a bridge to end a terrible nightmare. It came almost as a relief. He was weak and afraid to compete in the world he knew. He was afraid of the yellow-faced boys who would become men and fat doctors saying clever things like they did in college, talking fast and blowing cigar smoke, being successes. Beetlecreek was a womb. By some strange reasoning of his, he wanted to be gripped completely by death, wanted to be completely trapped. He was afraid to go on by himself.

Only once afterwards did he see outside this circle and that was when the child was born. He said, "Now I'll see that *he* doesn't get gripped by it, but I'll see that *he* is a free man from the start and I'll keep him away from darkies until he's strong enough to resist the death." And he made plans and made plans. But the kid escaped all this in the best possible way because it was born dead.

■ CHAPTER THREE

H E FOUND Bill Trapp seated under a tree repairing a wheelbarrow. It was the first time David had seen him since the night at Telrico's. Already, entering the gate, he felt freed from the cloudy fears that had choked him inside the church. Unmindful of the muddy ground he stretched out under the tree.

"I've been to Mrs. Johnson's funeral," he said, when he saw the old man staring at his clothes.

"I seen the hearse and all passing."

Bill Trapp started to go into the shanty to get something for them to drink but David stopped him. He didn't want to destroy the peace of the moment. He felt very strange, a soft warm buzzing inside. He felt religious as he hadn't felt inside the church. He thought of the child of his born dead.

"You sure you don't want some of that dandelion wine?" the white man asked anxiously.

David didn't answer at once. He stared for several minutes right into the man's eyes. He thought, You've been here all these years all by yourself and what do you know about it? You've built a wall and wouldn't look out; here, it's peaceful and quiet, what do you know about it? They threw stones at you, but did you suffer? Were you strangled?

"I could get it in a minute."

"The Reverend told about you giving those pumpkins for the church festival."

"That was sure nice of him but it wasn't nothin." Bill Trapp was smiling broadly, he kept licking the top of his gums as if to lubricate the smile.

". . . said you showed the real Christian spirit, that it's more blessed to give than to receive. At the barbershop they talked about it too. Slim, he's the one-legged guy that writes

84

numbers, was saying how surprised he was. The way they're talking now, you're the best white man in the valley. They change quick here." David chuckled.

Bill Trapp didn't say anything. He looked up at the sky. When it began to rain, they went into the shack.

"You aren't sick are you, starin into the corner like you're in a trance?" Bill Trapp put a bottle of wine on the table and shoved a glass in front of David.

Rain began to pour down, striking against the window, filling the room with a leaden light. Bill Trapp raised the shade so more light could enter the room.

"I want to do right," the white man said as soon as he had swallowed his wine. "I know I ain't exactly friendly and all, but I mean to do right."

He leaned over toward David and put his hand on top of his.

"That night you took me to the café was the first time I been outside with somebody in God knows how many years."

David looked away and withdrew his hand. He liked the old white man, recognized him as being good in a way few people he had ever known were good; but there was a smell to his breath, a smell like the air coming from a rotten log; there was a moldiness about his shirt, about all his clothes.

"I mean I'm very glad to see you again, Mr. Diggs," Bill Trapp said awkwardly. "I could tell you a thing or two about bein alone in the world, not havin nobody, just talkin to yourself all day. I could tell you a thing or two. And I want you to know I appreciate goin to the café with you that night."

David was embarrassed. "We'll go again sometime," he said, looking away to the road. He didn't mean it.

"That boy of yours been out here to see me. I like visitors. Maybe you think I didn't act like it all these years. But I mean to tell you, Mr. Diggs, a man gets used to bein by hisself and it ain't easy breaking habits. He's a fine boy, that Johnny of yours and if you see him—course you see him—but you tell him to come on out. He's always welcome."

David swallowed his wine in one gulp. Already he was feeling restless. Inside the wall with the white man, he felt hemmed in as by the walls of a cemetery. He'd had that feeling the very first time he'd come, as if he was entering into another world, a world of death and peace. If he could cancel this day, he thought, could block it out. Suddenly he wanted to see Edith! She was not of this world; she was alive and moving.

"I was tellin that Johnny about it," Bill Trapp was saying, "about how I wanted to open up this here place to the kids. Let em run around and have a good time. I never had no good time when I was a kid. I never would of chased them out in the first place only they was breakin the trees, and I mean to tell you when you're all alone it ain't easy to just do things like other people. I could tell you a thing or two about being alone all these years, Mr. Diggs."

David was thinking: But could you tell me something I don't already know, about the Death of this place? What is it you can tell me? Then he heard the man saying:

"I'm going to have a picnic for them first just to get it started. Those little white girls are coming and those Tolley girls. Going to buy the doughnuts up at the day-old bakery. They're cheap there but they're good; goin to serve cider in paper cups. Did Johnny tell you about it?"

"No," David answered. "But this picnic? White kids are coming?"

"Sure they're coming." Bill Trapp looked at him, an expression of complete astonishment on his face.

David thought, Uptown they have separate Santa Clauses at the Salvation Army Christmas Party. But why should he tell the old man about this. Maybe it would work.

Outside, the rain was falling quietly. A patch of pink sky gave a false illusion of warmth in the room.

"When are you going to have the picnic?" David asked. He felt very tired. There was no way to explain to the old man how complicated this story was, how Negro life was a fishnet, a mosquito net, lace, wrapped round and round, each little thread a pain . . . too complicated.

They heard automobiles stumbling over the muddy creek road. "It's them coming back from the cemetery," he said. He pictured her standing over the grave surrounded by black dressed figures hovering together under umbrellas, a little apart from them, perhaps without an umbrella herself. She would be standing very straight, taller than they, taller than their mock sorrow, taller than the grave—and, all around them in crooked rows, the white heads of other graves.

86

It began to rain harder, but now he must leave.

The old man held tight to his hand, too tight. David pulled it away almost rudely.

"I could tell you a thing about being out here all these years. You come back now, Mr. Diggs. I can see you're a gentleman. I know a gentleman when I see one."

David waved and, almost running, went back to the village.

When he arrived home, soaking wet, he found Johnny sitting in the unlighted living room looking out the window at the rain.

Mary, who had had only a half holiday for the funeral, had already returned to the Pinkerton kitchen.

"Some day!" David said.

"Some rain," Johnny replied, adding, "but I don't think it'll last long; the clouds are too low and fast moving."

While he was upstairs in the bathroom, David realized that in all the time his nephew had been with them, he had never had a real talk with him. They were strangers. It would be several hours before he could safely go to see the girl; he would talk to Johnny.

When he came down to the living room again, Johnny was still staring out the window. Something about the way the boy was hunched, poised as if to spring cat-like through the glass, made him stop at the foot of the steps. For the first time he noticed how thin the boy was, how sensitive were his features, and what sadness there was in the way he leaned his cheek against his hands as if caressing it.

He entered the living room and sat in the darkest corner.

"What is it, Johnny?"

"Nothing . . . why?"

He waited a while before he spoke again, then . . .

"How was your mother before you left?"

"Oh, she was all right. She was glad to get in at the county home instead of Hobb's Clinic. Hobb's Clinic treat you something awful but the county's good. They have shows come there and they have teas on Fridays when visitors come. Hal Reese told me, and his grandmother was there."

"I should of written her, but you know how it is. Tomorrow you and me'll write a letter to her together, you want to?"

"Yeah. O.K." But there was no enthusiasm in Johnny's voice.

"You don't feel bad, do you?"

"No, there's nothing wrong with me."

"Well, how come you're so quiet sitting there all by yourself. You want to go to the show?"

"No, there's nothing I want."

"Do you like it here in Beetlecreek?"

"Not very much."

"Aren't there any kids your own age to play with?"

"I guess so, but I don't like them. They aren't anything but down-home spooks." Johnny pouted.

"Well, what did you do with yourself in Pittsburgh?"

"We'd play ball and sometimes I'd read, but here they don't play ball very much, only basketball, and I can't play that and I don't feel like reading much."

David sat quietly and watched sheets of rain sweep across the street. The house became very quiet as the silence of other rooms joined the silence of the living room.

Then David knew that Johnny was crying. So ashamed was he, that he pretended he didn't hear. The boy's crying cut deep into him and he remembered pains of many, many years ago, boy pains and boy sorrows. And, understanding Johnny's sorrow and feeling it, he became one with him, and his hands tightened as he strained to hear every sob, every sucked in breath. And the past was very strong inside him.

After a while, Johnny got up out of his chair and left the room. David held his breath until the door upstairs slammed, then, silently on tiptoes, he climbed the stairs and stood on the landing, straining to hear the boy's crying. He trembled and choked from holding his breath. The excitement of secretly hearing the boy's crying was tremendous and thundering. To keep from breathing through his nose, he opened his mouth. He kneeled in front of the door and inclined his head toward the crying, straining, straining.

The past flowed through him and he was in the woods looking at a broken bird's egg, and he was in a railway station lost and surrounded by scraping feet and strange high faces and the terrible choking of steam engines, and he was alone in the big bed surrounded by the black space of the attic from whence came noises and moving lights, and he was looking from behind a bush at a gay party of finely dressed children. . . .

Suddenly the crying stopped and he was aware of his awkward position. And, frightened lest someone see him in that ridiculous pose, he jumped up and scrambled down the stairs to the living room where he sat once more in the dark corner, breathing heavily through his nose.

They had made no agreement about it so he wasn't sure she would come, but shortly before ten o'clock when Telrico's had begun to vibrate with noise and excitement, she appeared in the doorway, still wearing the tight fitting black suit she had worn at the funeral. Telrico bowed as she passed and others, glancing at the black suit, moved out of her way.

Only with difficulty had he managed to keep the booth free. Earlier in the evening Slim sat down beside him, boring him with a complete account of all numbers played that day which had come within two digits of hitting. By remaining completely silent he was able finally to rid himself of Slim's company. Later, Wilson sat opposite him, dropping clumsy hints and insinuations about the night David walked out of the café with the girl.

He was depressed. The sudden realization that his nephew was unhappy, the sudden realization that Johnny's unhappiness was in fact his own, the sudden opening of the wound of his childhood in Pittsburgh, all filled him with a sadness that broke off his feeling for the present, churned all of Now into a diffused dream and made even his desire to see the girl a senseless desire, having no real significance except that he had no control over it.

"You didn't come to the cemetery," she said.

"The church was enough."

"Yeah, I know. I wouldn't have gone to either one. . . ."

He wished she wouldn't say these things. They made him ashamed and clouded over the inner image he had of her. He needed to think of her as the girl of his college days, made beautiful by a sweet and melancholy sorrow.

She noticed his expression.

"What you need is a drink," she said.

They ordered beer and began drinking without looking at each other.

"I didn't ask her to adopt me," she said defensively. "I didn't ask her to buy me clothes and send me to college. All of them sitting there on their backsides looking at me and looking at the coffin as if I did it. I didn't ask her to bring me to this dump of a Beetlecreek. I got away as soon as I could. What did they expect me to do, these bastards?" She looked around the room at the people staring at her as if, at any moment, she would spit at them.

It unnerved him to see her hysterical. "How about another beer?" he asked. Her hair was uncombed and covered with yellow lint.

"How about a shot of whiskey?" she countered.

He could tell she had been drinking before, could smell it on her, could tell by the looseness of her expression.

"Telrico don't like whiskey drinking in here," David explained, "might get his license taken away."

"What a dump," she said, reaching for two empty glasses from the booth next to theirs. She poured the whiskey in plain view of everyone.

David drank his down all at once, but she drank hers slowly, gargling it about in her mouth like a mouthwash.

After a while, she said, "When I went to take a last look, it looked just like her mouth was moving. I swear her mouth was moving. Suddenly I thought she wasn't dead and almost fainted."

"Give me another drink," he said, handing her his glass under the table.

"You should have come to the cemetery. You're the only one in this town I give a damn about. Why didn't you come to the cemetery?"

"I told you why I didn't come." He thought she was talking too loudly. A couple from the other side of town—the headwaiter from the George Hotel and his girlfriend—stopped talking and were straining to hear their conversation.

"I know what you said," Edith retorted, "but why didn't you come? All those country apes looking at me like I killed her or something."

"I think they just like to go to funerals," he said. "I think they envy you, that's what I think." He lowered his voice almost to a whisper, hoping that she would take the hint. Already he was beginning to feel dizzy.

"That's exactly what it was," she said, "a picnic! A big picnic! They didn't really care anything about her unless it was Mrs. Ross who used to take care of her after I left. These good church ladies get on my nerves. If there's anything I can't stand, it's a good old church lady."

"But Mrs. Johnson really was a good person as far as I could see, lot better than some of them hangs around the church."

"Sure she did a lot of good things. She was always doing good things whenever she thought somebody was looking or whenever she thought she was storing up riches in heaven. I knew her, I tell you. I knew what she was. I lived with her for fifteen years and knew her inside and out!"

"Let's go outside," David said quietly.

He held her arm as they passed Telrico and the crowd around the bar. He didn't care now who knew about them.

They walked alongside the creek, past the swinging bridge until the road narrowed into a kind of path ending in the village dump.

The tottering derrick of an abandoned oil well dominated the field. They sat on one of the tar-soaked timbers that formed the base of the structure.

"I'm sick of cafés," she said.

"A man could hardly make it around here without Telrico's."

"Here—right here in this field—it's nice, like a good hotel room, like a good rug."

He took her hand and they sat quietly surrounded by the tar pitch smell and the faraway buzz of traffic in Ridgeville.

"This junk yard used to be bigger than this," she said, looking around her, "used to have new junk in it from all the drugstores uptown. I used to come here at night all by myself just to make Mrs. Johnson think I was out fooling around . . . when I was sick she would sing to me. It was nice when I'd get sick. She'd sing to me and be so kind. Then it was like she was my real mother."

He watched fascinated as she talked. Now he saw her as the girl of the college days. There, in the night of the junk yard, closed off from the Beetlecreek world, she had come back, and he recognized her and desired her.

She said, "Let's go away—you and me—go away. . . ."

91

At first he didn't understand what she meant. "Go away?"

"Yes. We could go to Cleveland or Detroit. Leave this stinking hole. What do you want here, what is there?"

And without answering her, he realized with a sudden flood of understanding, that this was the question—never asked, never permitted into his conscious—which flowed at the bottom of all his discontent. And with the question, was the answer. What *was* there for him in Beetlecreek? An occasional job painting signs, his wife and her ragged, faded pink slips, Telrico's . . . the death of the place. Was the death-grip, the absolute fear of movement or change, all that he had left?

"You could get jobs making signs for night clubs," she said. "I know them all, Harlem Grill, Cotton Club, Detroit Elks. . . ."

She was excited, hypnotized by her own words. She clutched at the loose folds of his trousers.

He tried to kiss her and was so clumsy that when she turned her head away, he fell backwards over her.

"Don't," she said.

He was ashamed and began sweating under the armpits. He rubbed his fingers over his lips; they were dry and crusty. His feet felt sweaty. He needed a bath.

She had moved to the edge of the timber. Her silhouette was taller than the edge of the bushes and her head was against the sky. Her eyes looked straight ahead. He thought she saw something and turned his eyes in the same direction, but he could not see what she could see.

She sat very still with her hands clasped in her lap. He knew the strength of her, the separateness of her, the queenness of her. He felt weak, pulled by her. He knew she was stronger than he. Sitting there on the edge of the plank, she was boss of him and he knew that in her there was escape from one thing, but imprisonment into another. Yet, if only he could stay with her, could draw strength from her. . . .

She turned her head toward him. She was smiling. But it wasn't a coy smile or a warm smile, or even the gay smile from the college days. It was a new smile, one he hadn't seen before, but which he recognized immediately as the cold, evil, big city smile.

"What do you think I am?" she asked.

"I don't know what you mean." The more he licked his lips, the drier and crustier they became. They were like two sandy lumps to his tongue.

"You know damn well what I mean, all right. What do you take me for?"

"I don't know what you're talking about. I swear I don't."

"You think just like the rest of them think, don't you?"

The moon butted through a formation of after-rain clouds and suddenly they were no longer closed-in in a junk yard, but were sitting in the very middle of a large, sweeping field.

"You think I'm just somebody you can pick up and play around with, don't you?" She turned completely about, straddling the plank to face him.

Now he understood what she meant. He remembered what his wife had said, "She'd give you a go if you went up the streets of the city."

"You're crazy," he said.

She looked at him, still smiling. "You're cute," she whispered.

"You know how I feel about you, how I've always felt about you. Why do you say things like that?"

"I just wanted to know. It's gotten so I don't trust nobody."

She jumped up and stretched. "Let's go back to town," she said. "It's past my bedtime."

He wondered if she were angry, but he was afraid to ask the question. To have something to talk about, he told her about his visits with Bill Trapp and of the old man's plan to have a picnic for white and colored children.

When he finished, she said, "I don't trust a white man. I wish every one of them could be put on a boat and sunk. I hate a white bastard."

They were walking through the darkest part of the road, and, although he couldn't see her face, he knew by the bitterness of her words, that her eyes were narrowed, her lips stretched back over the teeth in an evil mask grimace, like the time she told him she hated Mrs. Johnson.

"Once there was a white man," she said, "used to follow me sometimes. Once he caught me when I was coming from the movie uptown, near the A & P warehouse. That was the first time for me. I was thirteen. I've never told anybody about it, but ever since I've hated every rednecked one of them."

David knew that there was nothing he could say to the girl to make her feel about Bill Trapp as he did. Bill Trapp was a white man, and there was no convincing her.

He walked along the road, hardly bothering to lift his feet. The girl had defeated him, had forced her strength upon him.

He was afraid of her, yet, more than ever, he wanted to be with her.

What if she should go away soon, without him—tonight, tomorrow? He felt grit in his throat as he tried to force the words to ask her. Twice he began and twice the words turned into half grunts.

They were almost to the village and were passing an abandoned auto repair shop with walls that were caved-in, paper thin boards. I've got to ask her, he said to himself.

"You aren't leaving soon, are you? Aren't going back to the city?"

"That depends," she said. "It all depends on what happens here." She took his hand and bumped close to him. "Sometimes I'm afraid. Other times I'm not afraid of anything. Some of the girls have girl friends. I don't have anybody, not even a dog. Still . . . sometimes I'm afraid." Her voice had become very small.

He took her hand and placed it under his arm. He was glad the streets were completely deserted. The square plots in front of each house seemed more spacious in the darkness. On some of the porches dogs slept and he could hear them growling.

CHAPTER FOUR

EVER since the funeral, Johnny had felt restless and look-for-something. It was a continuation of the way he had felt when he was on the bus coming to Beetlecreek for the first time. It was a very strange feeling—a kind of stuffed up tickling inside that wouldn't let him sit still or be satisfied doing anything.

For one thing, he felt entirely alone, entirely separated from everything—his life, Beetlecreek, the boys, Bill Trapp, his mother, Pittsburgh, that bird—everything. He was entirely alone. It was as though his whole life, everything that had ever meant anything, everything he had ever done, was coming to a head, just like a pimple, here and now. It was as if now it were all to take on meaning.

He felt as if he were waiting for something. Like coming to the movie too early and reading the advertisements on the fireproof curtain to kill time, knowing with a very comfortable feeling, that the main thing would soon come. Like the excitement when the lights first go out before the movie starts, like when the eye can see nothing but the red and green light of the fire escape. Like that moment he felt. Like that moment of being hung in the air counting to a hundred and not breathing—that's what he felt and it was a terrible feeling.

Less than two weeks now he had been in Beetlecreek and everything was crazy and mixed up. Nothing belonged to anything he knew. He couldn't remember anything or anybody from the Pittsburgh world. Everything was strange and foreign. Everything he did was frozen out there in front of him so that right after he did it he could look at the action, examine it and measure it, and say to himself how funny it was and wonder whether it really was he who

95

had done it. He was no longer Johnny Johnson of 1906 Wilson Avenue, Pittsburgh, Pennsylvania, he was someone else. He was some Johnny in Beetlecreek who was staying with his uncle who was somebody else in Beetlecreek. And Beetlecreek was a funny little place where strange things happened that he was part of but which were like nothing he had ever known before.

And this feeling of being stuffed up, tickling inside, was a powerful feeling that pushed him around the streets and made him look at people and himself, made him watch them move and say things, a powerful feeling which made him watch himself and listen to himself say things, as if he weren't in himself but was sitting on a hill watching himself do whatever he was doing. It was a wild feeling, a feeling of running and chasing and screaming. It was a lightning feeling, a fire engine feeling, a hurting things feeling.

Underneath it all, there was guilt. Guilt because he felt he should be doing something, should be going to school like the other boys; shame because he wasn't somebody else doing something somewhere else; shame because he wasn't strong enough to do something about the fire-engine lightning feelings.

He was all alone—separate from himself. In the evening and sometimes in the afternoon when the sunlight moved around to the other side of the house, he would be filled with a delicious sorrow. Wonderful songs came to his mind and these songs he would hum. He would move his hands as if he were leading an orchestra and he would hum all the parts of all the instruments and the melancholy of his music would be very satisfying to him, would say to him, This is enough, this is good. And he would make more and more music.

But the sadness was never enough. He needed something else, and what this was he didn't know. With the stuffed up tickling feeling, he knew he was heading for something. From the hill where he could sit watching himself, he knew he was heading for something.

Sometimes he thought, Maybe he really wasn't in Beetlecreek. He would close his eyes and expect, when he opened them again, to find himself on the hunky's hill in Pittsburgh looking down on Wilson Street. He would expect to open his eyes and find the broad shiny river there and the boats and the stacks from the steel mills. But he was here, was here in Beetlecreek and every time he opened his eyes, they opened in Beetlecreek. And the quiet of Beetlecreek frightened him. Not the outside quiet, because outside there were Beetlecreek noises, faraway noises or unimportant animal talking noises, but it was the inside quiet, the waiting for something he knew not what that frightened him.

Everything he had done since he arrived in Beetlecreek had the feeling of being an episode in a dream. Everything he did seemed disconnected with the thing he had done before, seemed without relationship to anything that had come before or anything that would come after. Yet he knew it was all leading up to something.

First, there was his arrival at the bus station—the quiet, dead still, slow-dust-falling bus station. How, as soon as the bus driver shut off the motor, the Beetlecreek quiet wrapped itself around the bus station and he had to step down into it. How, putting his feet on the ground, he could feel that stillness and that quiet. That was the beginning of the dream, was the beginning of being separated.

And soon after, there was the time when he was with the gang of boys and was caught by the old white man. Even with all the excitement of being caught, there had still been the dream feeling about it all. Even his running over the grass was like running in a dream, like trying hard to lift his legs high and fast only to discover that they are feathers blown high and slow from underneath. Everything after that was puffy and feather blown, everything changed. The night he went to get his uncle from Telrico's and found Bill Trapp with him—that was feather blown and puffy, unreal, a scene from a dream. And it was as if he were on an escalator, riding up and up and up, riding toward something that was bound to happen. And, just like in a dream, he knew there was nothing he could do to help himself.

The time he was in the boys' shack was a dream scene too. That was a special day of dream feelings, strong, inside dream feelings, like when the Leader caught the baby bird and killed it. A strange way it had made him feel, as if he should try to kill something too. But there was also sadness for the dead bird and pain for the feather.

97

And in the barbershop had been a dream scene. He remembered how the fat barber held his head tight and asked how he wanted the sideburns cut. Sideburns were part of the dream because they made him think of how he would look when he was a grown-up man with his own automobile and many, many beautiful girls. But it made him ashamed that the barber should ask about it. It was as if the barber could read his mind and know what his secret thoughts were.

Even his uncle was part of the dream, his uncle who was such a strange man, a solitary, untalking man whom Johnny couldn't say anything to, in front of whom Johnny felt even more separate and embarrassed. Seeing his uncle was like spying on somebody because he knew the secret of his uncle. He knew his uncle was a sad-feeling man who perhaps was alone and in a dream too. Seeing his uncle was like recognizing someone in a dream and trying to yell at him but being unable to make a sound.

He didn't know what to do with himself. Sometimes he wished they'd made him start school even though he had come late.

He tried to read and when he was alone in the house, he would look at old magazines his Aunt Mary brought home from the Pinkertons', leafing through them backwards, examining the advertisements, especially the ads that said, DO *YOU* WANT TO MAKE MONEY?!! All of these he would read through carefully, closing the magazine when he was finished to dream of how he would spend the money.

He would buy a long, black car and in this car he would take a trip to Mexico and would attract all the beautiful señoritas and drive them around. And he would buy himself fine clothes and would drive the football team around in the car and be their manager and maybe buy them brand new uniforms with real shoulder pads.

And for a long time he would sit elaborating this dream until he went outside to be caught up in the outside dream again. Then he would walk along the street, keeping close to the fences and touching them, dragging sticks along the dusty road.

For many days now Johnny had avoided the boys in the gang. The day of the funeral, Baby Boy came up to him and asked him where he'd been hiding. Johnny told him he'd been busy but that was a lie. The truth was that he was ashamed to see them. He feared their scorn, imagined they had branded him a sissy because of what happened at the shanty.

He had the vague feeling that somehow he had failed a test and for that reason would no longer be suitable for their company.

Once his aunt sent him to the store uptown to get some groceries she had forgotten to buy. He was panic-stricken and walked all the way up the side of the hill over the railroad bridge so that he wouldn't have to pass the gang.

Twice they played whist under the street light near his window and he could hear their yelling. That same night, he imagined hearing one of them say his name and a lot of laughter afterward. This pained him very much and he turned over on the pillow so he wouldn't have to hear their shouts.

Another afternoon, someone knocked at the door while he was all alone in the house. When he went to the door he discovered that it was Baby Boy. He was overjoyed, yet he opened the door only a crack, not daring to let him in the house. Baby Boy wanted him to come over to his house to look at the pigeons. Very much he wanted to go but he was afraid of seeing the rest of the gang.

The night before the funeral, he was left all alone in the house. His uncle had given him enough money to go to the movie but instead he had gone to the A & P and bought a fifteen-cent package of buns with the money. After cutting through the alley behind the store, he climbed the hill that overlooked the valley and the creek.

On the hill, it wasn't quite dark but the valley was already covered by a dusty blue darkness. From up there where he sat, the creek was only an emptiness, a ditch. To one side of the village he could see Bill Trapp's place. There was a single, feeble light burning and even as he watched, the street lights along the creek road went on. From that height, they seemed like a string of weak Christmas tree lights.

The wind blew on the top of the hill and rattled the cellophane wrapper of the buns. He sat crouched with the buns in his lap. Two of them he ate, consuming them rapidly in a few big mouthfuls. It was so quiet, that the sticky chewing sound seemed to come from somewhere outside himself.

Soon it became dark on the hill and the valley below him

became level. The sky seemed close to the bushes. For a long time he sat very still, listening to the wind rattle the cellophane, listening to the sealed-in sounds of the valley rise up slowly along the grass.

What was it he was waiting for, he kept asking himself. What did he want? He tried to laugh to see if he could, but when he opened his mouth, the wind blew it away before he could hear it, and he could only feel the laugh on his taut lips.

He thought of girls. He thought of Little Orphan Annie. He thought of a picture in a magazine he had hidden among his things at home—an art photograph of an artist's model in the nude.

The wind blew harder and harder and tried to enter his consciousness and he could hardly breathe.

Afterwards, he ate all the rest of the buns and lay on his back looking at the sky. He was suddenly very tired. He closed his eyes and looked at the colored shapes behind his eyeball. This is all the world, he thought. The eyeball is the world. Maybe the world is God's eyeball. This thought amused him and he squinched his eye trying to make even more colors appear.

What was it he wanted, he kept asking himself. Where was he going? What was he waiting for? He tried to cry but no tears would come nor any sound.

He opened one eye and looked through a tuft of weeds toward the valley. I belong down there, he thought. I am down there and I live there. I am not in Pittsburgh but I am down there in the valley in Beetlecreek, and I am all alone down there.

What if Beetlecreek were a ghost town and he were the only inhabitant. What, if when he went back down to the street, he were to find everybody dead?

He wondered what the gang of boys sure enough thought about him. He didn't care if they did think he was a sissy, he told himself. They weren't anything but a gang of downhome darkies and he was from the city. But the thought of the shanty and the gang made him feel very sad. He was tired of being the weakest one in every gang he was in, the fraidy cat. In Pittsburgh, it was the same way. When it came to choosing up sides, he was always among the last to be picked.

And when it came to doing stunts, he was always the one who couldn't ever do anything.

He scraped his fist against the grass and pounded the ground. He felt ashamed of himself. Always he felt ashamed of himself and he was tired of this feeling.

Now he jumped up and ran down the hill. Recklessly he ran, taking a path that could only barely be seen in the reflected light of the moon. Once he tripped and fell. He wanted to cry, but he fought against it, shouting to himself, "You damn sissy! You damn sissy!" And on he ran.

Two days after the funeral, he had to take out ashes. His aunt said it wasn't good for a boy his age to have so much time on his hands.

So all that morning he carried out ashes, carrying them in two small buckets down to the fence behind the backyard and dumping them into the creek. While he was sweeping out the cellar, he remembered that he hadn't been to see the old man for a long time. Then he remembered that that very day the old man was going to have the picnic. How could he have forgotten!

As soon as he could leave his work, he went to the old man's house. He found Bill Trapp sitting on the porch looking at the debris left over from the picnic. At first he seemed sad and thinking hard, but then he began to smile.

"Where you been, boy? You're a fine one you are. Thought you were coming to the picnic. There wasn't nothing for you to be afraid of, them little girls was only about eight or nine years old."

"I'm just now remembering about the picnic," Johnny said, looking around the yard at the mess of pumpkin pulp and apple cores. "Looks like a good time was had by all!"

"They sure did have a good time! Nicest bunch of kids I ever seen, and got along together like they was friends all their lives."

Johnny sat down on the step beside the old man. Such a nice man, he thought, looking sideways at the old man's watery eyes. Such a good man, I bet he's like Jesus Christ. Johnny felt an overflowing warmness toward the old man and wanted to put his arms around him and hug him and be protected by him, wanted to be contained in the old man's kindness and goodness.

"What you looking at?" the old man said gruffly, jumping to his feet. "You wait here. I got some doughnuts and cider left over I'll give you."

Maybe when I grow up, thought Johnny, I'll be a missionary and go around saving souls in Africa or China and everybody will talk about how good a man I am and I'll make hospitals for the natives and maybe they'll build statues to me.

While they ate the doughnuts and drank the cider, the old man told Johnny about the picnic, breaking out, occasionally, into a high pitched laugh of delight.

"At first they were a little stiff," he said. "Acted like they was ascared of each other but when Mary Ellen and Sarah began laughing that funny cute way they have, wasn't no time before they were playing together as if they'd known each other all their natural lives. There were three of them white kids, all of them nice little girls. One of them was maybe not as nice as the others but she'll come around. Little girl called Pokey. I noticed her standing apart from the rest of the kids, not taking part in the games and everything so I asks her. Say, what's the matter you don't play the games? Said she just didn't want to be playing with no colored kids. So I left her alone, left her all by herself. You can't expect them to change overnight. Yessir, I just left her to herself and I bet you another time she'll be just as friendly as the other little girls. Once I went in the house while the other kids was playing and caught this Pokey looking into my anatomy book—that's a book that shows you how all the parts of the human body look. While I was standing there, wondering what I should say to her, she tears out a page from the book and stuffs it down the front of her dress. But I didn't say nothing to her. If she wants to learn about the proportions of the human body, I might as well teach her that as well as teach her how to get on with her fellow creatures. . . ." And he laughed a belly laugh that made Johnny laugh too. It made Johnny happy to see the old man so gay.

When Johnny finally left Bill Trapp, he felt entirely different. The man's kindliness and high spirits were contagious. Oh, what a nice man, Johnny kept saying to himself over and over again. He imagined the old man dressed in a long white flowing robe, walking very slowly and dignified over the country roads.

Johnny, himself, was carrying a stick, and he clasped it as if it were a Bible shepherd's staff.

So carried away by his thought was he, that he didn't see the two boys seated on the fence railing.

"Oh, oh. Look who's coming from the old fart's."

Johnny looked up, startled. He didn't know what to do. He was ashamed suddenly and wondered if they had been reading his thoughts. He dropped his stick and put his hands in his pockets.

It was the Leader and the boy with the red, scaly neck.

"What you been doin in there," asked the Leader, "gettin more pumpkins?"

"Hi, fellows," Johnny said, ignoring the question, ignoring their laughter. "I've just been inside looking at some of the guy's traps."

"What kind of traps?" asked the Leader skeptically.

"Watermelon traps," said the red-necked boy mockingly.

Johnny was defenseless before their laughter. He struggled to keep hold of himself. He spit elaborately and scraped a big T in the dust of the road.

The boys moved over on the railing and made a place for Johnny.

"We were looking for you the other day. We were goin up to old Hagan mine up on the other side of the hill."

"I've been busy," Johnny said. He could hardly believe what he had heard. They had been looking for him! Maybe they had already forgotten about what had happened at the shanty.

"Yeah, we know," said the red-necked boy, "hangin around the old peckerwood."

"No, I haven't," Johnny said, "I just happened to be passing here and went in."

"Well, if you know what's good for you and you want to join up with us, you won't be hangin around the white fart so much."

After a while, the Leader said, "We saw you at the funeral."

"Boy oh boy," the red-necked boy exclaimed, "did you see Baily Brothers' hearse. I bet that fart can go ninety!"

"Man, that hearse go faster than that. That hearse make a hundred and thirty easy."

"How come they make those things so fast? Dead folks ain't in no hurry."

"That's because they use them for ambulances, too," Johnny said, very proud to be able to contribute the information. "When my mother was sick, they carried her in one that was twice as big as Baily Brothers', all white with a back part that had three rows of beds. It was like a little room back there, even had a light over the bed."

Johnny didn't care that he was telling a lie. He didn't care that the dinky, wheezy ambulance from the county that came after his mother had been made of wood and had had barely enough room for the stretcher and the attendant, let alone room for three beds. He was glad that apparently he was one of them again, that no mention was being made of the disgraceful day at the shanty.

"When you guys going to the shanty again?" Johnny asked, trying not to sound too eager.

"We're going to roast taters maybe tomorrow. Why? You want to come?"

"Yeah. Maybe if I don't have anything to do. I've been busy."

"He's been busy!" said the Leader derisively. "He's been stayin in the house like a pansy and he calls that busy."

But Johnny was in too high spirits now to mind what they said. He left them and headed for home, singing "I'm Barnacle Bill, the Sailor" in a high falsetto voice and shaking his behind like a shimmy dancer.

"Well, canary bird, what you so happy about?"

His Aunt Mary was in the kitchen when he came in through the backdoor. He thumped his fist on the kitchen table when he passed. "I don't know, I just feel good."

"Well. I'm glad someone around here feels good. Those people up at Pinkertons' are enough to drive a person crazy. Don't know what's getting into that woman. Every time she decides to have a bridge party she don't say nothing to nobody and then wonders why there ain't no lunch meat in the house. Now you sit down here and eat something. You're getting to be as thin as a board."

Johnny helped himself to peanut butter and spread it thick on the slices of homemade bread already cut and piled on the table.

All Johnny's thoughts were centered on the possibility that he might become a member of the club.

"What you do with yourself all day?" his aunt was asking. "You be careful who you play with. I don't want you foolin around with that Wilson gang. They the very same ones that almost got picked up in the white people's part of town last Hallowe'en."

Johnny kept his head buried, pretending that he was concentrating on cutting his sandwich. What did she know about it? he thought. She probably wants me to play with that sissy Harrison that sings in the church choir and takes piano lessons. With those thick glasses of his, he looks just like an old bird.

"Next week they're having the Fall Festival and I'll be needing your help," his aunt said. "That'll give you something to do." She sat beside Johnny at the table and, leaning her head on her hands, looked out the kitchen window.

Her eyes are very young looking, Johnny thought. Her eyes stayed young while the rest of her became old. He had not forgotten that night when she sat downstairs in the dark crying.

"When are you going to start fixing for the booth?" he asked. He liked fairs and carnivals. He remembered the fireman's fair in Pittsburgh when he used to hang around the Bingo stand and guess which prize he would select if he won. He liked the low swinging lanterns and the lighted square around each booth. He liked the moths and the far-off sound of dance music mixed with the right-on-top-of-you sound of march music blaring out of the loudspeakers. He liked the whirring sound of the roulette wheel. All these things he liked, and the idea of a Fall Festival was part of the unsatisfied excitement he felt.

"Now, if you want to be a good boy and help me, we'll start on Saturday. You look down at the edge of the creek there in the alley and see what kind of wood you can find. Tonight there's a meeting of the guild and we're going to settle all the final details."

That afternoon when he was all alone in the house again and his aunt had gone back to Pinkertons', he wrote a letter to his mother:

Dear Mom, he wrote. I'm fine here in Beetlecreek. Everybody is nice. Next week there is a Fall Festival and I'm going to help Aunt Mary fix up a fine booth. She will make gingerbread and sell it for the church. She sure can make good gingerbread. Everybody says she is famous for it. There is a boys' club here and I am going to be a member of it. They are all good fellows and strong and do brave things. One of them has pigeons. They have built a club house and I've been there. I went with Uncle David to visit an old white man who is an artist. He is a nice man. He had a picnic for colored children and white children which was a big success. Now everybody in Beetlecreek likes him, but before everybody didn't and would throw stones at him. But he certainly is nice. I am fine here and don't you worry about me. I hope you are better now and everything is all right at the hospital. Love, Johnny.

He didn't go outside that afternoon. He was all alone. He sat in the corner rocker and rocked back and forth. He wanted to enjoy every minute of his happiness. He took the mirror down from the hall and held it so that when he stood in front of the full length mirror in the hall he could see himself from the back view. Then he held the mirror directly in front of the larger mirror and looked at the infinite number of reflections, one inside the other. I am inside of those reflections, he thought, inside each one of them there is me and I go back and back and back so that there must be billions and billions of me. Like a long path it is and I am like the trees alongside the path.

Then he looked at his face to see if he was really getting as thin as a board. He was very handsome, he thought. It always gave him the same short thrill looking at himself in the mirror as he received looking at pictures of movie stars. Certain soft lights made him look beautiful and made his eyes soft and like a woman's. Sometimes he would kiss his reflection. It made him very sad, his beauty in certain lights.

It was only two o'clock and he had almost two more hours to kill before the boys would be coming home from school. He went up to his room and lay on the bed. He fell asleep and when he awoke, he heard the late afternoon noises from out on the street. He heard the animal squealing of the grade school children coming home in the buses and he heard the hucksters who came to Beetlecreek last on their tour of town.

He jumped off the bed, went into the bathroom and

splashed cold water on his face, and changed into his old football jersey and leather patched trousers. Checking his appearance, he went outside. He would go to the swinging bridge and be there when the gang arrived.

■ CHAPTER FIVE

A LL DURING the meal, Mary was so excited that she could hardly swallow her food. David had finally painted the signs and they were safe in her bedroom where she had placed them beside the dresser earlier in the afternoon. She had made a special trip home that afternoon just to make sure they were still there and to look at them. Just before dinner, too, she had run up the stairs to look at them, holding them up to the sunset light, opening the window so the colors would shine. David had been acting so funny lately, she had been afraid he would get into one of his moods and refuse to paint them for her, but now finally they were finished and it would soon be time for the meeting.

The signs were the most important part of her booth. The gingercake, Lord knows, was important too, but there was no worry about it. At every Fall Festival as long as she could remember they'd asked her to make it. Leave it to Mary Diggs to make good gingercake, they'd say. But this year she wanted her booth to be the prettiest on the church grass. Prettier even than Mrs. Tolley's.

Mary had to admit that Mrs. Tolley knew how to make money. Mrs. Tolley with her fishpond sure was a moneymaker all right. Mrs. Tolley with her junky doo-dads for prizes could bring in sacks of money. Standing on that stool of hers, leaning way over the booth, her domineering torso and booming voice bullying children and grownups alike into investing their nickels—she could bring in money all right. But Mary told herself over and over again that if her booth wasn't the biggest moneymaker, it *would* be the prettiest. And to make sure it would be the prettiest, she was modeling it after one she had seen in the *Ladies' Home Jour-*

nal. Already she had made the apron she would wear that would match the colors of the booth—red, gold, and green. Mrs. Pinkerton had promised her a whole set of paper bridge napkins to give away with each purchase. Mrs. Pinkerton showed her how to twist crepe paper in a special way to make imitation roses.

This year, the Fall Festival was to be the biggest and the best. The depression is on, the Reverend had said at the last regular meeting of the Women's Missionary Guild, but there's still enough money around doing the devil's work to make this truly the biggest and the best festival in the history of the church.

The church owed the Reverend five months' salary and the guild hoped to wipe out the disgraceful debt through the proceeds of the festival. Colored people from as far down as Green Junction would come. They'd come in trucks and on the eight-thirty car.

The Biggest and the Best, was the motto (she repeated the magic words under her breath as she put bobby pins in her hair), and that evening final plans would be made.

She adjusted the belt to her gray flannel suit. It was her next-to-best outfit. Her best was a black satin dress with pleated bodice, but she was very proud of this suit. Hazel Pinkerton gave it to her before going away to college and now she wore it with pride, especially after the ladies told her it made her look five years younger. She chose her wide-brim Sunday hat to wear with the suit, the one, she thought, that made her look like the club women who came to Mrs. Pinkerton's Wednesday afternoon literary teas. She even put on lipstick, applying it roughly to the inside edges of her lips. When she was finished, she danced to the hall mirror and turned on the overhead light to inspect the final effect. She turned sideways and frontwards, assuming the various attitudes and expressions she would take when she was called on to make her report.

When she was finally satisfied with her appearance, she stopped in the kitchen where Johnny und her husband were still seated at the supper table.

"My, you look nice!" Johnny exclaimed.

"Yeah, what's going on?" asked David.

"Ain't I got a right to fix myself up sometimes? You all act like a body's got to dress like a ragamuffin all the time."

109

But in the hallway after she had said good-bye to them, Mary smiled broadly. Out on the street she still smiled, mincing down the sidewalk, hugging the signs close under one arm. Under the first street light, she stopped to peek at them. Bringing the signs to the meeting was a wonderful idea. Just having them there with her, knowing that they were all ready to put up, gave her all the courage she needed to stand before the ladies.

What dandy signs! she thought, squinching her eyes to see them better. They were painted in red, gold, and green to go with the colors of the booth and right through the middle was painted a banner bearing the legend: MARY'S BESTEST GINGERCAKE! Underneath was a picture of a fat man running, carrying a banner that said, First Come, First Serve! She had to chuckle at the expression on the fat man's face. There under the street light, she felt a very tender feeling towards her husband.

A single light burned in the church, a feeble bluish light so weak it was hardly able to penetrate through the imitation stained-glass windows. She ran up the steep concrete steps and opened the heavy door. Its creaking echoed and echoed around the cavernous room. Only the light over the altar burned. All the rest of the room was in shadow, like many smaller rooms in various degrees of darkness. In the hallway, she felt her way to the light switch and turned on all the lights in the church. The room diminished in size and the walls straightened up. The signs she placed in the closet where Mr. Ross, the janitor, kept his brooms.

Slowly and on tiptoes she walked down the aisle, very conscious of being in a church, very conscious of the fact that only a few days before had been Mrs. Johnson's funeral. Noiselessly she shuffled her feet over the worn nap.

Already there was a small fire burning in the giant cast-iron stove placed in the very center of the room, but she heaped coal upon it until there was a big blaze that flashed light through cracks in the bottom of its belly. She left the door of the stove open, enjoying the sting of the heat on her face and the crackling that destroyed the silence of the room.

Someone squeaked open the door. It was Mr. Ross. He came stomping down the aisle, his face screwed into a suspicious grimace. When he saw who it was, his expression relaxed a little.

"Oh, it's you is it, Mrs. Diggs? I was wonderin who'd be foolin around here so early. Knew there was a meeting scheduled but didn't expect nobody till nine."

"Just thought I'd come early to make sure everything was all set for the meeting."

Gently but officiously, he pushed her aside while he poked at the fire.

"Got to coax these here fires a bit 'fore they perk up," he said. "Coal ain't nearly as good as it used to be."

For five minutes he poked at the fire until it snorted and gave off waves of heat. Then he sat down beside her and the room became quiet once more.

Mr. Ross was a perpetually sad man whose hands shook and who was constantly wiping his eyes as if he were on the point of tears. For a while he sat hunched forward in his chair nervously fingering the handle of the poker.

"Don't seem like almost a week since they buried old Mrs. Johnson, now do it?"

"It sure doesn't," Mary said. She didn't like for him to speak of the dead woman while they were all alone. She didn't feel any particular sadness over Mrs. Johnson's death. As long as she could remember the old woman had been on the point of death. But she resented his recalling the funeral feeling she'd felt, because it clashed with the way she wanted to feel about the festival plans and the signs.

"You'd think the girl would show some respect for her mother instead of running around in cafés and carrying on like she's doin," he said.

"Well, you know that girl."

"I better go home," Mr. Ross said finally, "the wife wants to come to the meeting and there ain't nobody home to watch the kids. On my way out I'm going to turn out some of the lights 'cause we have to cut down on 'lectricity."

"Good night, Mr. Ross. Tell your wife to hurry."

For a while Mary amused herself watching the changing patterns of the greenish reflections on the ceiling. It was the first time she'd been off her feet all day and she allowed herself to doze. How good and comfortable, she thought.

She was awakened by the jostling laughter of a group of women. She recognized the voices of Mrs. Ross and Helen

Perkins. Quickly she rubbed her cheeks as if to wash them and straightened her blouse.

"Hello, chile, what you doin sittin there all by yourself in dark?"—"Ain't you the early bird," they exclaimed, seating themselves by the stove.

"Someone's got to be first," Mary answered gaily.

"Well, I sure am glad there's a fire tonight . . . getting just a wee bit frisky outside," Mrs. Ross said. She was a wrinkly faced woman who wore a tight stocking cap on her head instead of a hat.

Helen Perkins, who was with her, was a comfortable, fat-faced woman who taught in the colored grade school. She wore an exceedingly white powder on her face and two blobs of orange rouge in the exact center of her cheeks.

"You sure looks nice in that suit," Helen Perkins said to Mary.

"You just sayin, but I sure likes to hear it," retorted Mary in the peculiar whining tone of voice women assume when talking about each other's clothes.

Other ladies arrived and seated themselves in a semi-circle in front of the fire. They began chatting and scraping their feet on the floor until the room became noisy.

". . . so I told that Mrs. Bloom, I don't wash no clothes on Monday if I got to turn around do the same thing on Thursday. . . ."

". . . you right, gal, those white people sure run over you if you don't put yo foot down. . . ."

". . . hear tell she got married down at Charleston a year before she said anything about it up here. . . ."

". . . so the man told Henry down at the George Hotel, they goin start layin off the colored help if they don't start makin better service. . . ."

Mary got up and turned on the overhead lights. It was time for the meeting to begin, but Mrs. Tolley and Mabel White still hadn't arrived. Mrs. Griggsby kept looking at her watch and checking it with the time of the big clock behind the altar.

"I can't imagine what's keeping Amy," she whined. Mrs. Griggsby was the only one of the ladies who called Mrs. Tolley by her first name. She was a very light complexioned Negro with a sharp nose and nappy brown hair.

All the ladies looked around as if just noticing her absence.

Secretly, Mary felt very smug for having been the first to arrive.

"I can't imagine what's keeping her," Mrs. Griggsby said, "but we'll just have to wait."

Twenty minutes later when she still hadn't arrived, Helen Perkins suggested they begin. "It's way past ten o'clock and we've got a lot to do," she said.

"I think we should wait. She's never been this late before," Mrs. Griggsby argued.

"Nonsense!" whispered Mrs. Ross. "We ain't got all night. I make a motion we appoint a chairman and go on ahead with meeting."

"Second!" said Helen Perkins.

"Now how you goin second a motion and we haven't even begun a meeting properly," shouted Mrs. Griggsby, getting out of her chair.

"Well, all right, then," whispered Mrs. Ross. "I say we appoint Mary Diggs chairman."

"Second!" said Helen Perkins.

The other ladies enthusiastically murmured their agreement, and Mary was called to her feet.

Make her chairman! Mary could hardly believe what she had heard. She became alternately cold and hot across the breasts. Oh, my goodness, she thought. She must think of something to say. She was looking down at the floor. She must look up around at the ladies—smile!

Mrs. Griggsby had turned her back on the group.

"Don't see what all the hurry is about," she whined.

"Well, Mary, you're chairman. What you waitin on?" Helen Perkins was prodding her and smiling at her encouragingly.

"Well, now. I don't know what kind of chairman I'll make, but I'll do the best I can." Mary walked hesitantly to the center of the semicircle, smoothing down her slip. She smiled at each of the ladies, even at Mrs. Griggsby's back, and took a chair to lean on.

Many times she had practiced being chairman in the bathroom, and in Pinkertons' parlor while dusting, but now that she was standing before the ladies, she wondered if she would be able to go through with it. She was glad she had worn her club woman hat and the gray flannel suit.

"I guess you all know what the purpose of this meeting

113

is," she began. "I guess the first thing we better do is hear the reports from you all about the booths you all is going to have for the festival."

"We haven't even had the report from last meeting," interrupted Mrs. Griggsby again.

"This is a called meeting and you don't have to have the preliminary reports at no called meeting," Helen Perkins said.

A hush fell over the ladies. Mrs. Griggsby pulled her chair away from the group and flung her coat around her shoulders. "Some meeting," she sulked.

Mary rubbed the palms of her hands together. They were beginning to feel sticky.

"I guess we better go on and have the reports," she said weakly. She wished Mrs. Griggsby wouldn't complain so. She didn't like Mrs. Griggsby but she respected her. She had the feeling about Mrs. Griggsby she had about white people sometimes. Sometimes she thought she imagined Mrs. Griggsby even smelled like a white person.

"Maybe Mrs. Griggsby would like to give us a insight into her plans," she said cheerfully.

"I'm having the same thing I've been having for the last five years—a fortune telling booth—and as you all well know, it's been successful in the past, and it seems to me having all these here reports is a waste of time. What we need around here is a little more action and less of this planning nonsense!" Before sitting down, she flashed her eyes over toward Mary.

All the ladies who were to have booths made their reports. Helen Perkins said that she would have a girlie show in a tent and that when people went inside to look, they would see several ladies dressed in old-fashioned bathing costumes who would do a shimmy dance. The way she put her hands on her enormous hips and shook them to describe the dance, made all the ladies roar with laughter—all except Mrs. Griggsby, who pretended she wasn't watching.

Finally, it was Mary's turn.

"I don't know what you all will think of my idea, but I've brought an exhibit to demonstrate exactly what I have in mind," she said.

Walking down the aisle with the signs, her heart pounding, she kept them facing her so the ladies couldn't see them till the strategic moment.

But just as Mary was about to turn them so the ladies could see them, Mabel White came tiptoeing down the aisle.

"I'm sorry I'm late, girls," she whispered, taking off her gloves.

She took a chair and placed it in the midst of the ladies, blocking off any view of Mary's signs. This alarmed Mary, who thought that it wasn't right for anyone to sit where the chairman had to stand.

Mabel was breathing heavily and playing with her gloves.

"Well, girls," she whispered, throwing her head back knowingly, "you'll never guess what. . . ."

Mabel White was a loud-talking, silly-laughing woman who never whispered. Her talking could be heard all up and down the street. But now she was whispering.

There was something wrong. Something had come to take away from her the joy of being chairman. Reluctantly, Mary backed away from the center of the group and joined the other ladies who were staring at Mabel. She took the signs and leaned them on a chair in the back row.

"Something terrible has happened . . . poor, poor, Mrs. Tolley," Mabel moaned and whispered.

"What's happened to Amy?" peeped up Mrs. Griggsby, suddenly come to life, jumping to her feet.

"What is it, Mabel?" Helen Perkins asked. "Get yourself together and tell us what happened. Take your time, child."

Mary tried to imagine what it was that happened. From the way Mabel was acting, it must be horrible, something that had to do with Mrs. Tolley. Her first thought was that if something had happened to Mrs. Tolley, they would have to have the election sooner than the regular time, and who knows what might happen. There she was already standing before the ladies as temporary chairman. But it was indecent to think such thoughts. She tried to think of something else.

"Well, if you all will just give me a chance," Mabel said, in her normal loud voice, "I'll tell you what's happened." Then, waiting a few silent minutes and whispering again, she said slowly, "There's a fiend in our midst . . . a terrible, terrible fiend. . . ."

None of the ladies moved. All seemed to have suspended breathing. The stove door was open but there was no longer any flame. Helen Perkins put a shovelful of coal on the fire.

For a moment the red glow lit one side of the ladies' masks of waiting.

"I guess you all know this funny old white man lives out there on the May Place," Mabel continued. "You all know about him I know. Well, they tell me this man had a picnic yesterday and that Mary Ellen and Sarah was there with some *white* children. Little girl named Pokey was there, too —that's that family Doris works for up Windsor Drive— and that's how they found out about what happened. Seems like this Pokey took some kind of dirty picture away from the picnic and brought it home to show her mother . . . seems like there was some mighty funny doings out there. . . way I understand it, if you'll pardon the expression, the old man's *funny* . . . he was *molesting* the children. . . ."

All this Mabel gasped out in one breath. When she finished she began to cough.

"Well, I never!" exclaimed Mrs. Griggsby, sucking in her breath.

"Why, Mary, I do believe that's the same Bill Trapp that caught your nephew, Johnny," Helen Perkins said.

At first Mary was ashamed to remember that it was the same man. She imagined that this somehow implicated her in what happened, that it took away from her dignity as acting chairman. But she could tell from the way some of the ladies looked at her now—curiously, even enviously—that, to the contrary, she had won a new importance in their eyes.

"Yes, indeed, it's the same one," Mary said, "same one that gave those pumpkins to Mrs. Tolley, too."

"*Poor* Mrs. Tolley," the ladies chorused . . . "poor, poor child. . . ."

"Seems like he had all kinds of dirty pictures out there in his house, all hangin on the wall to tempt the young girls," Mabel continued, "horrible pictures of things would make them blush down at Telrico's . . . I can't even imagine what all . . . and if this little Pokey girl hadn't of took one of them home to her house, they never would of found out about it."

Mary didn't quite understand what molesting meant, but she could tell that whatever it was, was awful and unspeakable. Now that she thought about it, there *was* something funny about Bill Trapp. Something mighty mysterious about him living out there all by himself in the woods. She re-

116

membered passing him on the street. There *was* something funny about the way he looked at her, something very different about his eyes. Wait till her husband hears about this.

"And to think he's been living out there amongst us all these years," Mrs. Griggsby said, buttoning up her coat. "I must go to Amy, she's all alone. The poor, poor child . . . her children victimized by a fiend. . . ."

All the ladies were getting out of their seats, and there was complete confusion. Mary realized with distress that she was no longer needed as chairman. Nevertheless, deep inside her, was a warmth of pleasure knowing that proud, straight-standing-up Mrs. Tolley was in difficulty.

"Come to me a sign," said one of the ladies. "I had a sign. I dreamed of fish and death, which means trouble and this is what it meant."

"The devil's loose and doing his work," old Mrs. Ross said. "He is among us and we must pray to heaven for power."

"And to think he's been living here among us all these years."

"A soul ain't safe these days. I read in the paper only last week about a torso killer that sliced the bodies of his victims into little pieces and hid them in a trunk. . . ."

"God help us if this man would decide to do something worse."

"What could be worse than molesting the poor little innocent ones?"

"Helen is right, there isn't anything worse than destroying the innocence of the little ones."

"Someone should advise the authorities," Mrs. Ross suggested.

"That's just it," Mabel White said. "They don't want no publicity. Those white people don't want no county police stickin their noses in this mess. *Know* Mrs. Tolley don't want no policemen."

"No, indeed. No! No! they *sure* don't want no county policemens knockin at their door. It was terrible when they had that raid at Telrico's a few years back."

Mary didn't know what she should do. There was no use going on with the meeting. The ladies were putting on their coats getting ready to leave.

Mary herself was filled with intense excitement. Too many things were happening. She could hardly wait until the next

117

morning when she would go to Pinkertons' and find out what they were saying in the white part of town about it. Besides, Mary had a special relationship to what had happened. Hadn't her own nephew been caught by the old man, and hadn't her husband been out to the old man's place several times to talk with him? These thoughts thrilled her. All this brought her very close to what had happened and she felt very important, almost as if the tragedy had struck in her own home. It was as if she were in a very close seat to something that was happening, close enough to touch it if she wanted to, far enough away to leave it alone.

Helen Perkins walked home with her.

"What do you think it means, Mary? What do you think?"

"Don't rightly know, but it's terrible. . . ."

It tickled Mary to know that the devil was there among them. Knowing that the old man had looked at her funny like, made her feel as if she possessed secret information about him.

"What do you think will happen, Mary?"

"I don't know, but something has to be done to protect us from the evil power and influence of this man," Mary said firmly, very proud of the phrase, *evil influence*. "Our lives are not safe from day to day with that kind of fiend in our midst." She wanted to say sex-fiend, but she couldn't bring herself to pronounce the words.

"And only last week, the Reverend praising the man for giving those pumpkins for the festival."

"It only goes to show," Mary said, "that you cannot necessarily trust the giver of gifts, you can never tell when there is an anterior motive."

"I feel so sorry for Mrs. Tolley," Helen Perkins said.

"So do I," replied Mary, and she tried to sound sincere.

They were standing at the gate. The street light out front of their yard was broken and it was very dark. Mary didn't like the idea of entering her house alone. Not a light was burning. David was probably at Telrico's, Johnny must be asleep.

The talk of a torso killer made her uneasy. Near the steps was a lilac bush that formed an empty hole of shadow over the doorway. She fought the notion that a torso killer might be lurking there.

When Helen Perkins left her, Mary ran onto the porch and

broke into the hall as if she were being followed. Immediately she pressed on the hall light and the light in the kitchen and sat at the kitchen table, facing the door, waiting for David to come home from Telrico's.

■ CHAPTER SIX

THE SHALLOW, mud water of the Beetle Creek, the ever-so-gently creaking swinging bridge, and the mainline railroad tracks, all separated Beetlecreek from uptown. The creek curled around itself to make almost an island of Beetlecreek. The swinging bridge was narrow and made out of ancient, tar-pitched planks. The Streamliner between Washington and Cincinnati whooshed through the valley twice a day without stopping, a silver streak with a new style train whistle—not really a whistle at all, but a long, amplified sigh. All this separated uptown from Beetlecreek.

Uptown they were talking about Bill Trapp. Uptown, especially in the pink-roofed part, they were talking about the old white man who lived in the darkie part of town. During those days, white kids from the pink-roofed part of town, whenever they could get up enough nerve, would take walks along the creek just to see where the old man lived, kids who had never been in the colored part of town before. They would walk in twos and threes, sometimes young girls with them, holding hands, the girl feeling safe in the company of the young swain, both feeling the need of courage to come so near the house where the old man lived.

Sometimes in the walking, they met small groups from Beetlecreek who were walking to see the same sights, walking to get the same thrills, and the two groups passing each other would stare curiously at each other. But the colored group wouldn't hang their heads or lower their eyes. They were proud and honored to have the white people there, nevertheless, making it clear by the way they walked, familiarly and unhurried, that this was their show and their offering, something that happened in their village.

All those first days, maids and bellhops and waiters hustled

120

across the bridge, back and forth nervously, bringing news and communiqués of the latest developments in white people's homes, bringing tales and information back to Beetlecreek, fanning the air, spreading out the welcome excitement, making it last as long as possible.

Once, many years before, there had been a raid. The county police rode into town that night in their red-starred Fords with the radio antennae swinging back and forth like important batons. Drove up and pulled up in front of Telrico's so fast no one knew what was coming off, smashed up the gambling fruit machines and carried off Telrico and drunk old Harry Perkins before people could hardly figure out what happened. That was some excitement but it had happened many years ago and had all worn off. This Bill Trapp thing was the first big excitement since then, and everybody was ready.

Fifteen years now he lived in the old May Place. That first day when it was known that someone was moving in, there was a lot of this excitement. It was something like that this time, that is, there were groups of slow walking people, promenading people, talking quietly and speculatingly among themselves.

Fifteen years he lived there without saying hardly a mumbling word to anyone. Fifteen years, and people figured that something should have happened. So there were the stories about the strange lights and the strange noises, and stories about the way things grew inside the fence.

And during all this time, the old man, Bill Trapp, just stayed inside his fence where he could be seen by spooners of a Sunday afternoon, sitting on his porch rocking, or standing under one of those gnarled apple trees of his, looking out toward the road. Sometimes, once a week about, he could be seen pushing his wheelbarrow uptown to get supplies. But mostly he kept to himself.

Fifteen years and then this thing happened, but it was about time. Fifteen years was a long time to wait.

At the barbershop, Slim said (he was counting pennies and they were spilled out on his lap), "I been just waitin for something like this to happen. White man don't live around colored people unless he's wantin somethin from them or got somethin up his sleeve."

And Mr. Tolley, for whom the excitement was a thing that

made him open the barbershop almost a half hour earlier every day, agreed with everything that people said about what happened. Actually, he was proud that he was so closely involved, proud that his shop was a kind of central information booth. It was at the barbershop, the day after the ladies got wind of it, that the men first gathered to discuss the thing and so stamp it official.

At least five times that first day he was called upon to repeat the story just as it had been told to him by his wife, adding, of course, whatever details he deemed necessary for dramatic emphasis. One time, for example, he said the picnic had been an orgy. His wife had called it an orgy, repeating the word that one of the madams uptown had used, and he liked the sound of the word.

Tolley, himself, would have liked to have had the story printed in the newspaper. As it was, one of the men at the Elks who sent reports of lodge activities to the Negro newspaper, promised to send in an article about it.

But Tolley readily agreed that it would be disastrous to have anything appear in the white paper.

"We don't want no publicity about this thing," he told an out of towner, "we don't want the little ones' names defamed."

The day he had to go with his wife to the house of the white girls to discuss the matter with their parents, he was very proud. That morning, he closed his barbershop at ten o'clock and dressed himself in Sunday black. Later that morning, still dressed up, he appeared in the barbershop and told them what happened.

"Well, sir," he said, fastening the apron over his black serge suit, "those white people sure are worried about this scandal, but they're willing to let bygones be bygones as long as they has a guarantee that the old man don't molest no more children, but they don't want no officials from the county messing around with the case, if it means testifying in court and so forth. I assured them that I would cooperate fully with them in the matter, because naturally I have to look out for the interests of my own little girls."

Bill, the shoeshine boy, watched everybody who entered the shop. If someone entered who he thought hadn't yet heard the details of the excitement, he would be on pins and needles until he could steer the conversation in that direction.

"It's getting so a man ain't safe in his own backyard," he'd say casually. "Now take this here white man, Bill Trapp, been livin in our midst for going on fifteen years, ain't said a word to nobody, ain't had nothin to do with nobody and he takes a notion into his head to have this picnic and commit all these immoral acts."

If the visitor showed no interest or not enough, Bill would make another explanation in which he would use the word "sex-fiend."

"Yessiree," he would say, a serious cast to his face, "you'd never suppose lookin at this quiet valley, we got us a real honest to goodness sex-fiend in our midst, would you?"

Several times that first day, Slim said indignantly, "Now you turn the tables of this thing. Make like there was a colored man lived all by hisself in a white part of town and he gets it in his noodle to bring the races together just like he's Jesus Christ, and I don't believe that was the reason to have the picnic in the first place, regardless of what that Diggs is goin around sayin, but just play like he did want to bring the races together and it was a colored man livin in a white town, and he starts all this monkey business with white girls mind ya, what do you think would happen to *him*? You just pick up any newspaper from the last few years and read what happened to them Scottsboro boys and you can imagine what'd happen to him! His life wouldn't be worth a row of pins I mean to tell ya—not one row of pins!"

Whenever Slim would say this, the men sitting on the waiting benches would stir uneasily, would squirm in their seats as if they had the bites. Slim would see them squirm and would aggravate their uneasiness. What if there *had* been a colored man instead of a white man?

Once the idea was said, had entered into the conscious and the way of thinking about the thing, everything changed; the balance, the color, the sound changed so that in a day or two, it became a steamroller.

All of a sudden, the idea was there for everybody to see, plain as day. What if the old man *had* been a colored man. The idea was a big one and it filled the gray brown emptiness of those days between summer and winter.

"What if the old man *had* of been a colored man," mum-

123

bled school children, munching their lunches at the colored school. "What if the old man *had* of been a colored man," asked maids, leaning over white people's fences, watching white people's wash dry. "What if the old man *had* of been colored," they asked in Telrico's over beer, and at the barbershop while they turned in their numbers.

Then came Sunday and the Reverend got up in church and shouted, "The devil's in our midst!"

"Amen! Amen!" they shouted back at him, for now everyone knew who the devil was and what he looked like, and it was thrilling to recognize the devil.

"The devil's here and we must protect ourselves," he shouted. "The giver of gifts need not necessarily be a good man. The devil does his work in clever ways. He's here and we must pray to Him above to protect us from him below!"

"Amen! Amen!" they chorused, and they meant it, for to have the devil there was a wonderful and fearful thing.

So that Sunday, when the people left the church, they thought about what the Reverend had said. They remembered how he had praised the white man for giving pumpkins to the church. Now they shook their heads in wonderment. The devil does his work in clever ways the Reverend had said, and this explained many things.

Mrs. Tolley wore mourning dress. Every day she wore black silk. With whomever she met, she discussed the terrible events, going into the greatest detail to explain how she never suspected the old man was *that* kind of man when she accepted the pumpkins. From morning till night she was in someone's parlor or kitchen extracting sympathy.

The two little girls, Mary Ellen and Sarah, were kept locked up in the house, not out of punishment or for fear they would get into more mischief, but because she didn't want them going around telling people that the old man was *not* an evil old man, but was a nice man who treated them very kindly. Mrs. Tolley knew they were either lying or were just trying to protect the old man. She forgave them, though, because she sensed the tremendous magical power of the devil. She imagined he exercised some power over them just as he had exercised some power over her and had tricked her into accepting the pumpkins.

Days went by, and the excitement, instead of dying away as it well might have, became more intense and joined up with the fall winds and the gathering of leaves and the screaming of migrating birds.

Then a strange thing happened; the weather became warm, a kind of Indian summer it was, and it seemed that some freak of nature had brought color and spring feeling to the village. Birds swooped and swooped through the chimneys and telephone poles, as if undecided whether or not to leave for the South, and earthworms came to the surface of the ground. Mid-day would be hot as summer day and evening was lush warm like July.

Boys began to play under the street lights and girls would be loath to go in at night. Chairs were brought out on porches where swings had already been taken down. Days passed and the wonderful summer weather stayed on and all accepted it.

With the coming of the freak summer, the Bill Trapp excitement increased and increased. Now, all who hadn't been for a walk down the creek road past his place took advantage of the warm weather to make the pilgrimage. Coming back, they'd stop in Telrico's for a bottle of beer or an ice-cream cup.

More and more the idea of the devil being among them seized hold of the imaginations of the people. Talk became big.

"Idea of an old white man like that carryin on those kinds of things," they said at the Elks during one of the monthly meetings. "What we ought to do, is investigate the thing and have a committee make recommendations to the body."

So, at the Elks, this was done, a committee was appointed. But days passed and the committee didn't function. There was to be a state convention and the committee, called the Bill Trapp Committee on Decency, promised to take a stand there.

Telrico didn't take part in the discussions going on around him at the bar of his café. Telrico was a white man himself, an Italian who lived in the back of his café. His wife and family lived over the hill in Munstor, and twice a week he and his son went to visit them. Nobody thought of Telrico as a white man, but he never forgot it himself. And he kept out of the discussions. Whenever someone would ask him his opinion, he'd just grunt and change the subject.

Those days of the freak summer were very strange, and

125

people began wearing summer clothing again. The sky was a funny lavender color and always without a single cloud. There was a shimmery electric feeling in the air as if the world were enclosed in one huge neon tube.

Definitely something was going to happen. The cold wind had blown the excitement into the valley, had blown the leaves, and made the birds swoop, but the cold wind had gone and left only the excitement and the freak summer. Something was going to happen and there was a waiting feeling about.

Especially under the street light in front of Telrico's where, as soon as the freak summer began, groups of boys of all ages began loafing. They would stand there with their hands in their pockets or they would play mumblety-peg. There would be complete mumblety-peg tournaments. The craze to play the game began with the freak summer and lasted up to the night of the festival. Games would begin early in the evening and last until after Telrico's closed, when drunks would gather about and place bets. Once Telrico tried to break up the mumblety-peg tournaments. He said their noise would attract the county patrol car, but the games began every night on schedule in spite of his protests.

There were specialists and champions in mumblety-peg and almost every boy in the village was there watching or hanging around because of the waiting feeling in the air. This was the season when there should have been touch-football games or basketball games, but there was only mumblety-peg.

Dogs joined the excitement under the street lights and made water on the fence posts nearby. Girls came out and sat on the roadbank, laughing and giggling among themselves, knowing that they were being watched and measured, wearing tight sweaters that showed their fourteen-year-old development, dancing among themselves, shouting back clever rejoinders to the smart alecks playing mumblety-peg.

"You sure looks good to me, Lucinda, with them fine things stickin out in front. . . ."

"Don't you Lucinda me, boy, I knows what you needs. . . ."

The birds swooped and swooped, all the time screaming, undecided what to do. The freak summer fooled everybody and everything.

"Hadn't been anything like it in years," said the old folks. All the time, waiting was in the air. The mumblety-peg tournament went into its third big night. Some people brought out their swings again.

■ CHAPTER SEVEN

JOHNNY sat on the railing of the swinging bridge looking down toward the creek. He leaned over and spit, watching the curved path the white blob took before hitting the water. The cold wind pushed the bridge back and forth, back and forth very gently and the greased cables strained against the big holes in the planks.

He rattled the buckeyes he had in his pocket and decided he would make a buckeye pipe. He looked for a nail with which to clean out the pulp. If he waited until the gang came by from school, he could borrow the Leader's scout knife, but it would be a good half hour before they came and he was nervous and excited.

While he was bent over, looking for the nail, he saw a familiar figure walking slowly toward him. At first he wasn't certain and remained stooped over to make sure. He squinted his eyes; yes, there was no doubt, it was Bill Trapp.

Johnny had tried hard to shut out any memory of Bill Trapp ever since that first morning when his Aunt Mary told him about what had happened and had forbidden him ever going to the May Farm again. But even before that, he'd had a feeling that Bill Trapp belonged to that part of his dreams where things happen in a flash without reason, changing color and shape to fit whatever was going on. Yet he hadn't been successful in trying to forget Bill Trapp, because, while he never talked about him to anyone, not even to his Uncle David, and while he shut his ears to what people around him were saying, the ragged edges of terror remained inside him to torment his sleep and render unreal his day.

But what should he do? It *was* Bill Trapp and before long he would see Johnny. What should he do? He couldn't face the old man, couldn't face those eyes. He must think of something to say.

He thought of ducking under the bridge, but decided he had already been seen. There was nothing he could do but wait.

Now the terror that before had been at the bottom began to rise. He was afraid of what he might say to the old man, was afraid of the way he might act in front of him. Surely the old man knows already what people are saying about him! Johnny had heard the man called monster and fiend, and, though he knew the old man was neither of these, the very fact that people were saying these things changed already the feeling he had about him.

Most of all, Johnny was afraid to stand before the old man's eyes. He was afraid to have the man look at him, inside him, to see what he was thinking, he was afraid to have the man read his thoughts and spell out the words, monster, fiend.

At first, Johnny had laughed to himself at what they were saying about Bill Trapp. He knew of the picnic from the very beginning and so did his Uncle David. He knew that the old man would never do any of the things people were saying he did. But that was it! No one was making any specific accusations. No one knew exactly what had happened, except that it was something awful and "dirty." Johnny had heard them talking about molesting and had heard them say something about sex-fiend, and while molesting didn't mean very much to him, sex-fiend did, and right away he had thought about the old man's deep-set lavender eyes.

All the fiends that Johnny had ever seen were only movie fiends. There were vampires like Dracula, and monsters like Frankenstein. Bill Trapp, except for his eyes, didn't look anything at all like either of these. Really, the old man looked more like a Sunday school picture of a saint.

"But you can never tell in what kind of form the devil appears in our midst," his Aunt Mary had said, and he thought about this. What about the uneasiness he had felt with the old man at first, what about the time the old man looked at him in the eyes for almost fifteen minutes straight without saying anything that first day? How come the old man decided to be nice to the people after all those years of staying by himself?

129

Johnny was puzzled by all that was going on and he was tired, tired of explaining to himself the meaning of all that was happening to him. He felt as if he were caught up in something and was twirling around and around like the Crazy Wheel at the amusement park and that at any moment he would be thrown off into something terrible.

He hunched on the railing of the bridge, his back turned away from the direction in which the old man was coming. He could hardly breathe. When he stuck the nail into the buckeye pulp, he tried to concentrate on what he was doing, but he could hear the footsteps coming nearer and nearer.

He thought of running, getting up and making a dash for it. He thought, If I get up now, I can just make it to the bend in the road. He found himself wanting to cough and spit. He began rubbing his knees together as if to still the urge to run.

The nail, he took and threw into the creek. Then he threw the buckeye away. He thought, If I could swing down over the railing and land on that little sandbar underneath . . . looking down made him dizzy. He felt a bitter fluid rise in his throat and when he spit, there was a taste like vomit in his mouth. He slid down off the railing and leaned against the telephone pole at the edge of the bridge. Without looking, he knew that the old man was almost to him. He stopped breathing, waiting for Bill Trapp to speak. His eyes were wide open but he could see nothing. He concentrated all his senses on the man's coming.

After what seemed a very long time, he knew that the man was standing behind him.

"Boo!"

Johnny started.

"I guess I scared you all right, sneakin up on you like that," Bill Trapp said, giggling.

With all his strength, Johnny tried to move his face muscles so that he would look surprised. But he knew that there was nothing on his face but fear.

He tried not to look at the man's eyes, concentrating instead on the frayed edge of his collar. Finally, he felt as if he could speak. "Hello, there, nice day, isn't it?"

"What you doing here all by yourself?"

"I was just waiting on some of the gang," he managed to answer.

"I thought you'd be coming out to see me again. You sure you ain't waiting on some pretty little gal?"

He tweaked Johnny on the cheek and Johnny jumped back as if he had been slapped. He began shaking all over and felt as if he were dropping apart.

"What's wrong with you, boy?" the old man asked.

Johnny couldn't answer but just stood looking into the old man's eyes. If he could only get up enough nerve to run.

For a moment he thought he was going to cry. A great gripping and ungripping swelled up inside him. He opened his mouth to breathe and blew out. Then he became calm. Suddenly and unexplainably, he became calm. He coughed and sat on the railing again.

"I thought you wanted to come out and see some more of the traps. I've got some dandies put in where the creek back waters."

What should he say? He couldn't say that he'd been ashamed to come because of the stories about the picnic.

"I—I've been busy I guess."

"You've found you a little gal. Well, you can't blame them, a fine looking boy like you. I'm going uptown to get some things. You ain't seen none of them girls around, have you? Promised they'd be coming back and ain't none of them showed up. Like to see that one that stole the picture out of the book, that Pokey. Wonder what she's doing." He giggled.

Suddenly it all became clear to Johnny. Pokey was the one who started all the stories. The "dirty" picture was the picture torn out of the anatomy book!

He started to open his mouth to tell the man, but his mouth refused to open. Then Johnny remembered that the boys would soon be coming. What if they would see him with the man?

"You don't want to go uptown with me, do you?" Bill Trapp was asking him.

"Oh, no," Johnny replied, trying to make his voice as friendly as possible, "I can't go uptown because I've got to meet my aunt here . . . but I'll be coming out to see you, don't worry."

"Oh, God! Oh, God!" was all Johnny could say as he sat on the railing, watching the old man walk toward town. At first he was filled with remorse for not having told him about the stories, but he was so relieved to be alone again, that he

131

could do nothing but breathe and breathe. Besides, he told himself, he knew nothing of what went on at the picnic.

The Leader was in front running and the other three boys were jogging along behind him. As soon as he was close enough, the Leader threw his pocketknife at the tree beside the bridge.

"Some throw," Johnny said.

The gang all crowded around Johnny panting. "You sure is lucky you don't have to go to school," one of them said, "that fart gave us a test already."

"What you do all day?" the Leader asked, pulling his knife out of the tree trunk.

"Nothing. Just loaf around." Johnny was proud to be able to say it in just that way.

"Well, you sure is lucky."

They stood there throwing stones at bottles. Johnny was anxious to go to the shanty.

"How about going to the shanty?" he asked, trying hard to pitch his voice just right so they wouldn't think him too forward.

"You ready?" the Leader asked. "Then, what're we waitin for?"

This time Johnny led them with a fast trot which developed into a race. Johnny won easily and was proud and happy. For the first time he felt himself to be a member of the gang, felt eligible and equal.

"Boy, my leg's givin me all get out; that fart of a charley horse givin me the devil," the Leader said, making an extravagant show of massaging his leg.

When they arrived at the shanty, the Leader unlocked the door and stood by while Johnny entered first.

They sat on the floor and lit a candle. The light was low on the floor and made the ceiling seem high as in a church.

For a long time they sat quietly around the candle, cupping their hands over the flame to make shadow pictures on the ceiling. They seemed to be waiting for something.

Johnny knew that, sooner or later, they would ask him about Bill Trapp. But now he was ready for them. No longer did he feel responsible and involved in what had happened. Now it was something that he could talk freely and openly about.

Then the Leader asked him, "What do you think of your buddy now?"

"What buddy?" Johnny asked, knowing perfectly well that they were talking about Bill Trapp.

"You know who we're talking about—that old peckerwood you're always hanging around with, you and your uncle."

For a moment of panic, Johnny thought they might have been spying on him when he was talking with the old man. But they couldn't have, he reasoned, since almost a half hour went by before they had appeared.

"Oh, him, Bill Trapp? I haven't seen him for ages."

As soon as he said it, Johnny knew that it was all finished between him and the old man. No more would he go to visit him. As far as he was concerned, he had never known him in the first place. He was a little afraid now that he had told the lie, but he didn't care. He felt reckless.

He felt free, too. Like he felt sometimes in school after having finished an important examination. He looked around him at the group of boys and smiled comradely at them. We're all one gang, he thought, we'll do all kinds of exciting things together. He felt like embracing each one of them and snuggling closer around the candle. He felt as the Indians must have felt, a circle of braves gathered around the council fire. He took a deep breath and held it so his chest poked out. He wished he had cigarettes to offer them.

"Now you play like that old peckerwood was colored and he pulled a trick like that," the red-necked boy was saying. "You know what'd happen to *him*. They'd string that fart up so quick."

"That's just what ought to happen to this guy," Johnny found himself saying indignantly. He was surprised to hear his voice. It was his voice, all right, but . . .

"Wonder what the old goon did?" one of the boys asked.

"Lots of guys like them young." It was Johnny's voice again.

"He must be crazy."

"That's just it," Johnny's new voice said again, "that's what makes them like that. He tried some funny business with me once, but I told him off."

The longer he talked, the more he began to believe himself. He felt as if he were an entirely different person and it was a wonderful feeling. It was exactly like having a brand new suit of clothes, the same You but an entirely new cover.

He took one of the cigarettes they offered (this time they had a brand new pack of Chesterfields) and stuck it in his mouth like he had seen it done in the movies, his eyebrow cocked, his lower lip drawn far to one side.

"Thought you didn't smoke," the Leader asked him.

"I was kidding you guys," he answered. "I been smoking ever since I was nine years old."

"I thought you was kiddin," Baby Boy said.

The smoke made him feel funny in the stomach but he fought against being sick.

"Let's get the meeting on," the Leader said.

Baby Boy took his place against the door as guard and the others moved in closer around the candle. All of their faces became stern and they poked out their lower lips as if in determination.

Johnny was excited as he had never been before unless it was the time he had to raise the flag all by himself in the Flag Day exercises at school in Pittsburgh.

"Give the sign," the Leader commanded them, and they all bowed their heads and put their hands on each other's shoulders. All of them except Johnny, who couldn't participate because he wasn't a member yet. He moved a little behind them and bowed his head anyway, making a kind of cross on his chest as he had done the time he went to a Catholic church with a friend of his in Pittsburgh.

They were mumbling something under their breaths that Johnny couldn't hear. Baby Boy at the door was doing it too.

Oh, if only he were a member! Finally they straightened up.

"Nightriders," the Leader was saying, "we got a lot of things to do, but first, a lot of you guys ain't paid your dimes and we don't got much money left over from the last feast, so if you guys want to stay members, you better get ready to pay your dimes."

Johnny slitted his eyes and looked straight into the flame of the candle. All this is a strange thing, he thought. Now I am different. I have felt myself change. I am someone else. Right here in this shack, I have felt myself change. I am no longer the Johnny Johnson of Pittsburgh, but I am another Johnny, here in this shack, I am another Johnny. Here we are, all joined together, comrades seated before the council fire, and I am seated here too. This is better than anything, this is the most important thing I want. To be a member of the gang and do wild, brave things together with them is the most important thing I want.

The shadows of the boys seated before the candle danced clumsily on the ceiling in bloated pantomimes of their movements.

The last time Johnny was in the shack seemed like a time from his childhood, remote and dim lit. He remembered the bird and the way he had run away as though it were something that had happened years before.

He even imagined he felt different physically. He could feel his arms and legs as if they were stronger and thicker. He bundled his fingers tightly into a fist and flexed his muscles. He put the palm of his hand on the floor and deliberately rubbed it back and forth to dirty it. He was far away from the meeting in a land lit by the glow of fires. There were many warriors.

Later, they told him that if he wanted to become a member of the Nightriders, he would have to be initiated and that they would tell him when. Baby Boy whispered to him soon after that he would be called one night late and would be initiated then.

This excited Johnny very much and he imagined being awakened late at night to answer some mysterious summons.

After the meeting, when they began looking at the dirty pictures, Johnny joined them, the new Johnny.

Boldly and frankly, he looked at the picture of Little Orphan Annie and Punjab; coldly, and without appearing too interested, he looked at the picture. And when he was a turmoil of crazy feelings inside, he sat in the dark corner with the rest of them.

Nor was he ashamed later. He told himself, This is the new Johnny, it's all part of being together with the gang.

Only once did he think of Bill Trapp. The Leader had proposed that they go out to the May Farm and swipe some apples. Before Johnny knew what he was saying, he had said, "Oh, you don't have to swipe them; he said you could get all you wanted just by asking for them."

They looked at him coldly. One of them laughed. Johnny felt ashamed and pretended he had to scrape something from the sole of his shoe. He remembered how the old man had looked at him that afternoon sitting in the sunny quiet of his porch, how he sat rocking back and forth, pushing the hair out of his lavender eyes, a kind, funny smile on his face as if he were laughing at some secret joke.

But he pushed this image out of his mind, quickly and completely, and once more he was the new Johnny.

The door was open now and the candle had been blown out. Now the shanty looked less dramatic. The walls were uneven planks full of holes and splinters. Daylight shone through the joints in the corners and ceiling. In one corner was a dung-colored hornets' nest and there were spider webs, dusty and bedraggled, hanging from the boards above the doorway.

He left the boys at the swinging bridge. He could hardly wait for the initiation. He wondered how he would be notified. Maybe, late at night, one of them would throw pebbles at his window like they did in a movie he had seen once. Or maybe they would hand him a slip of paper with a map drawn on it.

His house was empty when he arrived home. He went into his aunt and uncle's room and closed the door. For a few minutes he lay very quietly on the bed. Then he got up and pulled down the blinds.

In the semi-darkness, he thought of the new Johnny. He repeated again, I am a new Johnny here and I will be a member of the gang.

He turned on the little pink-frilled lamp on the dressing table. Mixed with the daylight streaming in from under the drawn blind, it made a diffused, peach colored light. This was the light that made him beautiful.

He took a hand mirror from the dresser drawer and looked at himself. He half closed his eyes until the lashes came together, pretending that he was asleep. This is the way I look when I am asleep and it is very beautiful. Then he turned the mirror so that he could see himself sideways. I could be an actor because I have a beautiful profile.

Then he smiled at himself and raised his eyebrows as if he were surprised. "Why, how do you do? What a pleasant surprise, madame. . . ."

Then he smiled at himself again and moved his face close to the mirror until his lips touched.

For a long time, he lay on the bed exhausted. He wondered when his aunt and uncle would come home.

He dozed off, and when he awoke, he awoke with a great jerk. A strange tasting fluid was in his mouth and his throat felt tight. "Bill Trapp!" he said. What am I thinking of him for?

But he could remember no dream about the old man, yet, there he was in his thoughts. He was afraid. He felt scattered again. The armor of the new Johnny had turned to dust and he was full of doubt and fear.

With a great sickening feeling of guilt, he thought about that afternoon on the bridge when he had talked to the old man.

He felt as if he were being watched. He jumped off the bed and threw up the blind. The flood of light in the room didn't change the funny feeling he had, so he ran down the stairs and sat on the porch.

Now it was evening but there was a strange hanging in the air. There was a cloud of milk colored light in the atmosphere making it seem as if the night didn't want to begin. It was warm, warm as spring. He felt the warmth and saw the unusual light and wondered about it.

The warm wind blew up from the railroad tracks and filled the yard with a smell of spring dampness.

■ CHAPTER EIGHT

BILL TRAPP was a man who was dead, had brought himself back to life again, who once more longed for the known groove of death. These thoughts in different shapes came to him as slowly he walked through an alley on his way back from the store in Ridgeville. It was a narrow alley, full of overflowing ashcans and puddles. The roofs of the houses slanted uniformly and each well-kept back fence was painted white. There were groups of small children playing marbles in those places where the ground was dry. They were white children who did not know him and who only raised their heads to give him a passing glance. But he walked close to the garages on the opposite sides of their games, because once again he was filled with the oldest feeling he had ever known. He was ashamed.

Ashamed and afraid. The dream that he had built up of flimsy hopes and awkward gestures since the day that boy, Johnny, had come to him was not strong enough. It was too old, this feeling; the weave of it was too tight. He was an old man now, and tearing open the layers of petrified sorrow, forgotten and strong, ripping them open and letting light touch the cowering soul required a hand stronger than his.

This he understood when he looked into Johnny's eyes on the bridge. The boy had been afraid of him. And though he tried to ignore it at the time, he had had the same message at the picnic. Like a light at the end of a tunnel he had understood. It was a blinding fright which he had felt, a blinding fright which toppled over the too hastily constructed framework of the dream and·filled him with the longing for escape and forgetfulness.

Because he had lied, first to himself and then to Johnny

about the picnic. It was not a success. The colored girls were afraid all during the picnic and would hardly speak to the little white girls. He had understood immediately what they felt, though it surprised him to know that even with them there could be the same childhood terror he had known, the same feeling of shame to be in the world, the same need for shadows and dark places to hide. It immobilized him, this realization, filled him with sadness that stretched back to his own childhood. He watched helplessly while the little white girls, the ones who had first come to visit him, approached the colored girls asking them pretty-please wouldn't they join the games; but the little colored girls, holding tight to one another's hand, only shook their heads and kept their eyes lowered. He had had to serve the cider and doughnut refreshments much sooner than he had intended to because he wanted to cheer up the little girls.

There was one girl at the picnic who hadn't been invited. This girl, who was ugly and tall, was called Pokey. He had heard her snicker at the colored girls' pigtails and heard her call them jigabooes. The colored girls smiled at this, he remembered, but after that they hardly breathed or moved. Pokey said she had to go to the bathroom, and while the other two white girls played with him, she went behind the shack to the outhouse. For a long time she didn't come back and this worried him so that he went into his house to call her.

Then he saw it: there peeking under his pillow was Pokey! He watched her, at once fascinated and horrified, as she lifted his covers and smelled under the rough, ragged sheets. He held his arms very stiffly to his sides so as not to make noise breathing. He watched her spit into his washstand and make a face at his mirror. She went to the dusty bookcase and leafed through several of them, afterwards wiping her hands on the sheets. One of the books held her interest, however, and he watched motionless while she tore a page from it and stuffed it down the bosom of her jumper. She turned then and looked into his eyes. He flushed. There was in her eyes a look of raw human hatred such as he had never seen before and he was frightened. He ran out the front door and did a dance for the children in the middle of the pumpkin patch. Then he lit the pile of leaves under which he had placed a box of fire powder and waited for the explosion. Brr-ooo-mm! it came, scaring away two flocks of birds, making a great puff of red smoke.

Shaking hands good-bye with the children, he was unable to look into Pokey's eyes. He gave each of the girls a basket of apples to take home with them and they were all smiling. They promised to come back, each of them, but he knew that there would be no more. For a moment he stood there and he saw the little colored girls run ahead toward the village

Later that evening when he had shoved the memory of what he had seen far back into the recesses of his mind, he tried to tell himself the picnic had been a great success, that the little girls had had a wonderful time. Then it had been a necessity, but now the days had become too long again.

He began spending most of the day in bed. He would sleep late and go to bed early now; nothing held his interest. He no longer bothered to leave the house. He ate practically nothing; only occasionally would he scrape away the green mold from a doughnut and eat it dipped in canned milk. Then one day he went to town to buy food and that was when he saw Johnny. Once again he was afraid.

Returning from the store, he took a path that led over the hill so that he could enter into his property without having to pass through the streets of Beetlecreek. He forced his way through the brambles that crowded the narrow path. His head was bent and he carried the bag containing three cans of beans and a sack of cornmeal close to his chest, as mothers sometimes carry babies. The hill was steep and he breathed heavily. His brow was wrinkled because now another thought had entered his mind. He said to himself, What if I cannot go back to the old way? And what he meant was that it might not be possible. Life having been breathed into the lungs of the dead must be taken away again before death can be returned to. This thought filled him with panic. In the eyes of the little white girl, Pokey, in the look of Johnny, there had been a sign.

A cat slipped up to him in the dark and rubbed velvetly against his legs. "And what do you want, little cat?" he asked.

He put the cat in his pocket and took it home with him. He placed food before the cat but it wouldn't eat. He took an old hairbrush and brushed the cat's fur. This action soothed him and occupied him until he fell asleep with the animal in his lap. How would the days pass now? Once more he tried to read the books. He thought about Hilda and the peace of sitting on the back porch of the boarding house licking the vanilla cream from the waxy inside of the squashed ice-cream box. He thought of that day not long ago when he poured beer for the colored man in the back of the café and of how he thought it was the beginning of a new life for him that evening. He thought about the brown truck that the county sent for the Italian and in the same image he was on a train looking down on the flooded tracks at a dead horse floating with the slow current.

Time had stopped. There was no desire left in him. He had stopped moving, had achieved, in fact, that which at first he wanted so badly—complete equilibrium. He had come almost to the complete stop.

■ CHAPTER NINE

NOR DID David know what to make of the talk about Bill Trapp. Somehow, he couldn't get himself into a frame of mind to think about the thing clearly. Of course he didn't believe what they were saying. Yet, the whole wheel of rumor, the freak summer, and the complete disorganization of his own life with the girl, kept him from distinguishing that which was real from that which escaped from his nightmares to tear down the walls separating sleep from wakefulness.

Those first days after he heard what they were saying, he went about as in a dream. He refused to participate in what was going on about him. He entered into a voluntary daze, walking slowly from home uptown to Telrico's without really changing scene. Once his wife asked him what he thought about what was being said about Bill Trapp and he had told her, very angrily, that she should mind her own business.

Sooner or later, he knew that he would have to go to the barbershop to face the men, yet, he put it off as long as possible, at the same time prolonging the duration of the strange state he was in, a state of wandering, a state of ignoring that which had already bound him, chained him to what had already happened, to what would happen in the future. He knew perfectly well, even if he wouldn't admit it, that he was involved in what had happened at the picnic, had, in fact, felt the coming of it the last time he talked to Bill Trapp.

After two days of staying away from the barbershop (and in Beetlecreek, it was no easy matter to ignore the center of life that was the barbershop), he could no longer stand being divided into so many states of mind. And to relieve himself, to get it over with, he went to the barbershop on the third day.

But when he entered, there was no rioting, no immediate attack. All was quiet and calm, and there might not have been tragedy, so restrained was their greeting.

The barbershop was almost empty. There was only Slim, Bill, the shoeshine boy, and Tolley.

"I remember once back in 'twenty-five, stayed warm like this all winter," Slim was saying.

David sat in one of the vacant barber chairs and motioned to Tolley that he wanted a shave. The worn leather on the arms of the chair felt like old newspapers.

Tolley was putting on tennis shoes. "Well, last year," he said, "we had snow in September; you sure can't tell about the weather."

David knew that they were only stalling for time before they would say something to him about Bill Trapp. But he didn't care. Somehow, that fall morning, warm and tender as spring, all that had happened seemed far away and unimportant.

"We're putting up our swing, too," Bill, the shoeshine boy, said. "Had to throw off two blankets last night and sleep between the sheets."

"Makes me think of once during the war it got warm like this and flowers started blooming right in January," Slim said.

Tolley began lathering his face. There were no other sounds except Tolley's asthmatic breathing and the close to his ear crackling of the soap fluff. Slim pretended to be counting numbers slips. Bill was looking out the window and scratching his behind. David knew, by the way they were acting, calm and exaggeratedly at ease, that they would ask him now. He tried to anticipate what they would say. He was ready.

"Well, it happened just like I thought it would," Slim said. "You can never trust a white man."

"What do you think they'll do to him, Mr. Tolley?" asked Bill, the shoeshine boy.

"Well now, yesterday I went with the madam down to the girls' house, the white girls mind you, and we had a talk with the parents. They were very nice white people, very nice people indeed. Served tea and English biscuits. Well sir, we decided that it would be better all the way around if we didn't prosecute." Tolley reared back against the mirror

143

holding his dripping razor as if it were a magic wand. With one hand he covered David's forehead.

David lowered his head lower than necessary so the others wouldn't see his expression. When Tolley freed his head once more, he tried to look uninterested, as if he couldn't understand what they were talking about.

"Well, I say he shouldn't get off so easy. You know what would happen if a colored man would of done all them things. Just like I said before, there's somethin mighty funny about an old peckerwood livin around colored folks!" Slim rubbed the shiny material bunched up at the stump of his leg, indignantly.

"What do you think of all that's going on, Diggs? Seems to me you got a special interest in the old bugger, you always talking about how well he understands the race problem." Tolley looked around at the others in the shop and winked.

"Ha! Ha! ha-ha-ha!" laughed Bill, the shoeshine boy. "That's why he understood it so well—he *sure* likes the race . . . the race of little girls! Ha! Ha! ha-ha-ha!"

"Shut up, Bill! Let Diggs talk and quit actin a fool."

"I don't know, Tolley, I think things explain themselves," David said quietly.

He remembered how, that night, his wife was sitting up, waiting for him to come in from Telrico's, how every light in the house was on, and how, the moment he saw her face, he knew that something terrible had happened. She was sitting at the kitchen table and hadn't even taken off her coat. "The old man," she said, her voice hardly more than a whisper, "he's done a horrible thing."

At first, he hadn't known who she was talking about. Then, she said, "The old man who gave the church the pumpkins."

Ever since that day, he had hardly dared walk the streets. In the mornings, when he knew the streets were full, he found some excuse to stay indoors. At first, he made himself believe that this was only because he didn't want to answer a lot of foolish questions, but he knew, at the bottom of it all, was a feeling of guilt, as if somehow, even remotely, he were responsible for what happened.

That night he slept badly. He found himself repeating over and over again the story his wife had told him. He believed every word of it, while at the same time he fought against believing it. Several times during the night he pictured what the old man might have done to the girls, and he would begin shaking under the covers.

Johnny avoided him and he avoided Johnny as if they had an understanding about what happened and had made a silent agreement by which neither would speak to the other about Bill Trapp.

"That ought to teach you to trust a peckerwood," Slim said, smiling, spitting, stomping one foot on the floor to emphasize what he had just said.

David, seeing triumphant Slim, felt angry with himself for not, in some way, defending the old man. There must be something he could say. But he could think of nothing.

"Everybody can make a mistake about judging a character," Tolley said. "Used to be a bellhop at the George Hotel that had keys to everything in the hotel—everything I mean, safe, everything—everybody thought there wasn't no more honest darkie in the world, when one day this fool jumps up and steals about two pounds of bacon and they catch him."

"Ha! Ha! ha-ha-ha!" laughed Bill, the shoeshine boy. "Just like a darkie, just exactly like a darkie . . . white man now'd get put in jail for stealin a million dollars' worth of jewelry, but old shine goin get the same sentence for stealin two pounds of bacon. Ha-ha-ha!"

"What's all the laughin about, gentlemen?" Mr. Jim Anderson entered the barbershop and plopped himself into one of the chairs. "Hello, there, Diggs. Ain't seen you about for a while. Ain't been hidin, is you?"

"He-he-he-he!" giggled Bill.

"Now you cut out all that foolishness," Tolley said, trying hard to keep a straight face himself.

"Yeah, he's been hidin," Slim said. "His peckerwood buddy's in trouble and he's been hidin."

David was angry, but he tried to remain calm. "Everybody's entitled to make a mistake," he said, feeling very foolish for having said it.

"Well, all I can say," said Jim Anderson, "is that you made a mighty big one and a mighty serious one. That man's a fiend if I ever saw one and it's a crime and a shame that he's gettin off as easy as he is."

"That's what I say," said Slim.

"A *damn* big mistake," echoed Bill, the shoeshine boy.

That same afternoon, when he was sitting in the Johnson living room, he told Edith about it. The window was open, and the warm air was expelling the musty smell of the room. She told him the room hadn't been opened since the funeral.

She was dressed in the same black suit. He wondered if she had no other dresses. She listened while he told her the story of the picnic as he knew it, and of what they were saying at the barbershop. She listened quietly with her hands folded in her lap, but she seemed restless and uninterested.

"I heard all about it one afternoon at Telrico's," she said, "I heard the whole rotten story. They ought to string the bastard up."

"He might not have done all those things," David said quietly. It had never occurred to him before to doubt the old man's guilt, but now, confronted with the girl's bitterness, he felt the urge to defend Bill Trapp.

"You know what I think about white people, especially white men," she said.

"After all, there wasn't any proof. Nobody's got any specific information."

He remembered one thing the old man had said, talking about the days he was with the carnival, "The only ones worth saving are the kids," he had said, "it's the same about everything, the only ones worth working with are the kids. Ain't no use to try to make a trapeze artist out of a grownup."

It was a panicky feeling he felt sitting there in the solemn living room. On the wall was a picture of a Civil War battlefield with a regiment of Negro troops lined up stiffly to fight a white cavalry. On the piano top, there were framed photographs of church festivals, concerts, and picnics of years gone by. Scattered about the room were hymnals and church publications with dusty, yellowed pages. One booklet was called, *The True and Living God:* His Manifestations for the Good Baptist Mother. In the corner were two pots of ferns, forgotten by Baily Brothers.

Why hadn't the old man listened to him? He had warned him about the picnic. It was cursed from the beginning. He himself had felt it. He remembered how he had felt, in-

stinctively, the danger of interfering with things as they were
—even the Death of the village.

There were too many pieces of furniture in the room. He
felt oppressed by the curlicues and worn tapestries of the
old-fashioned pieces. Inside himself he felt oppressed by the
necessity to think about the things that were happening.

How happy he had been to have the girl come back, to
live again the college days. But secretly, he knew that
there was no reaching back to the past, no fooling around
with things as they were.

And it was this knowledge that filled him with panic.
There was no way, really, that he could shape himself. He
felt as if he were stepping off a path already cut out for
him, an easier path, by continuing to see the girl, by continuing to stretch out the dream of the past. He felt that
he had stepped off a path already cut out for him, too,
when he began visiting the old white man.

He remembered another thing, how, when he first entered the girl's house, that afternoon, she had been in the
hallway to greet him. There was a yellowish-green light that
shone like a spotlight down from the stained-glass window
on the landing. In that light, when she put her arms around
him and her face was close to his, he saw her as she
would look when she was an old woman. It was around the
eyes that he noticed it. The way the shadows were at first,
made her face seem young and beautiful as he remembered
it. The high curved eyebrows and the eyes slightly slanted
upwards, the thin nose, and the lips that smiled only in
the very middle, were all the same. But then she moved,
and he saw by different shadows, her mask of old age. Already, as young as she was, there were thin lines around
the socket of the eyes and just above the upper lip. The old
woman part of her was there, waiting impatiently to take
away the youth.

And this made him very sad because he knew that there
was no permanence in anything. He thought, if there were
some way he could go back to the way of living he knew
before, a complete resignation to the Death of the village;
if there were some way he could escape the panic feeling, the
feeling of having gone too far from known ways and known
paths, the feeling of having separated himself from the past,
he would have taken it willingly. By himself, he was afraid.

147

He had stepped outside himself by going with the girl, bringing life to himself when the village had already killed him, he had stepped outside himself by becoming friends with Bill Trapp, had upset the delicate balance of things as they were, had interfered with the smooth running of what had already been prepared for him. And by this interference, he had made it necessary for himself to act for himself. And sitting there in the dusty crowded living room, he was panicky, afraid.

He sat on the far end of the couch as if to shrink away from the thoughts that assailed him, as if to shrink from the crowded room and the girl, resting against the edge of the piano with her eyes closed.

Neither of them spoke. It became late afternoon. Twice the light had changed, once from the sparkling yellow-green of early afternoon to a whitish indoors haze, then to a dirty flannel color tinged by the sunset at the end of the street.

A warmish movement was in the air, not really a breeze from the open window, but more like an infinity of minute vibrations.

"I'm sick of this place already," she said. "They're all looking at me, not that I give a damn."

"There're strange things going on," he said, "I feel it. . . ."

"This place gives me the creeps. This funny summer in October. . . ."

"I knew something was going to happen, I felt it coming. . . ."

"Last night you didn't come to Telrico's. Out front, there were two cats fighting. . . ."

"Maybe Bill Trapp didn't do it, it's possible. . . ."

"Two kids whistled at me. There were gangs of them out front when I went in. They were still there when I came out and they whistled again. . . ."

"They might have an investigation anyway. The county might find out and send somebody. . . ."

"Then staying all by myself in this empty house. . . . Today, I looked through her things. There were old party dresses, almost brand new, old-fashioned ones like they wore in the gay nineties, and the bottom of the trunk was filled with ostrich feathers, red, purple—all colors."

"You'll be going soon, then?"

She looked at him as if just remembering that he was in

148

the room with her. "I'll never come back again," she said.

"People have lived here too long," he said. "No new people, all the sames ones, the same jobs. When Brady Mine was finished, so was the town, but the people stayed. They should have left when the company did."

"Bellhops and waiters and maids," she said. "Kids growing up to be delivery boys and old men with gray hair waiting tables and women dressing up on Sunday in clothes white people gave them. . . ."

"They've lived here too long. Beetlecreek's too old. . . ."

"Here, there isn't any change outside so you feel yourself changing inside too fast. You feel like there wasn't any reason to be here in the first place. Waiting tables is no reason to be here. . . ."

"Waiting tables is no reason to be here," he echoed.

"I'm afraid to stay, afraid to go. I don't belong here and can't stay because I feel like I've got to go somewhere else, anywhere. . . ."

He thought of the days when he would wander to the bus station to hang around and watch the flashy blue Greyhounds come in with their signs that said, Tampa, Washington, St. Louis, Buffalo. . . . He would go to the lavatory and put a penny in the machine and weigh himself and read his fortune, and for a long time he would linger in the whitewashed, lime-soaked atmosphere. He would look through the checkroom window at the bags, the smart new leather ones, and the imitation alligator ones from Kresge's. Sometimes he would pick up bits of tags and tickets and finger them a moment before throwing them away. Sometimes he would put them in his pocket and carry them around for days.

"Why don't you go away with me, even for a little while?" she asked.

"I could, maybe . . . for a little while . . . a week maybe. Just go. . . ."

"I've got enough money, I've got insurance money." She was getting excited and was walking nervously around the room. She kneeled down before him and looked right into his face.

It was the same light that revealed the old age mask of her. He could see each of the lines under her eyes, and the blue greasiness. But she was still beautiful. The old age

149

mask, if anything, made her seem stranger to him, more exotic. There was an old Jewish woman for whom he often painted signs, a woman who owned a dress shop. This woman, this Jewish lady, was beautiful in the same way. Often he would wait outside until she would arrive just so he could enter into the red plush of the shop and see her in the dim lights of the wall lamps.

"When would you be going?" he asked. "Soon?"

"I couldn't leave until Saturday," she said. "Is that too soon?"

Saturday was the night of the Fall Festival. "No," he said. "No, that's all right I guess."

PART FOUR

■ CHAPTER ONE

ALL UP and down the street, there was an awareness of
the festival. For that early evening hour, there were
more people than usual crossing back and forth across the
swinging bridge. Ladies, coming back to the village from uptown kitchens, carried mysterious pans covered with gleam-
ing white tablecloths, and they walked faster, nervously
like birds in the early morning. On their faces, were stretched
rubber-band smiles.

On the street there was a steady stream of traffic; important kids pulling toy wagons loaded with fifty pound
blocks of ice and streaked, marble-green watermelons, and
men, home early from work, carrying hammers and saws
and rolls of wire, all heading for the church grass where a
line of booths and a few strips of crepe paper were already
giving a gay, festive appearance to the raggedy grass lot.

Because of the strange hothouse warmth in the air, doors
and windows were wide open. There were women ironing in
the doorways, and excited big girls running back and forth
across the street with their hair greased into pigtails or shiny
balls.

It was absolutely an important day, full of a special
festive tenseness. But Johnny didn't feel it.

Even though he could see the festival taking shape around
him, Johnny didn't feel excited. Early that afternoon, his
aunt came home from Pinkertons' loaded down with three
huge pans of gingercake she'd baked on their electric range.
All day in the house there had been the smell of pink icing.
Uncle David had been in and out several times and had
spent part of the afternoon painting signs and price tags for
the various booths. As soon as school was out, kids began

chasing dogs into the church grass and running them round and round.

But all these goings-on didn't interest Johnny. He felt separate and apart from the festival. He could tell by the way kids broke up the everyday games of mumblety-peg and by the way they were dressed, in Sunday blue suits and Sunday frocks with some little girls already knotted up into shiny pigtails, that it was an important day of the year, like the annual Sunday School picnic. But he didn't feel part of it.

The night before, he dreamt that his mother tried to tell him something but couldn't because a great stream of vomit and blood came from her mouth every time she opened it. That same night, too, he thought about the team's raffle they had had the year before in Pittsburgh to buy jerseys for the football team, and it made him feel very lonely to know that they would be wearing the orange and black uniforms, and that he wouldn't have one even though he sold more chances than any of them.

And even though he tried to think of other things, he knew that he still felt a dismal, lost feeling about Bill Trapp. In some way, when he was dreaming about his mother, when there came over him a hot, melting urge to cry, he knew that Bill Trapp was mixed up with what he was feeling for his mother. In the dream, they were one and the same, and about each, he remembered feeling very sad.

Only sometimes was he the new Johnny. It didn't last when he was by himself. As soon as it became silent enough around him, he would know who he was. Only when he was with the gang did he feel strong and different—outside himself. But he hadn't seen the gang all day. He waited for them a long time down by the swinging bridge but they didn't come. And while he was there, he thought about Bill Trapp again. Feeling alone and neglected himself made him think of the old white man being all alone and neglected. He's there, closed inside the stone wall, all by himself, an old man, all by himself, he thought. And this thought amplified his own feeling about himself, and he wished he were away from the village, wished he were near his own hill, near the sound of the whistles of his own Pittsburgh trains.

And at the very bottom of these feelings, like the current

pushing the stones at the bottom of the creek, or like standing in the rapids and feeling the underneath strength of the water force you off balance, was the feeling of waiting, expecting, and coming-on. But this feeling was too big for him to understand or think about; he could only know that it was there.

That evening, he went home feeling downcast and lonely. Walking down the street, he was mindful of the movement toward the festival, and even when he saw the Dairybell ice-cream truck backed up at the side of the church, he wouldn't go to join the children watching the unloading of the ice-cream boxes.

He entered the house and sat in the darkened living room, thumbing through an old *Popular Mechanics* magazine. When his aunt called him to supper, he went without relish. He hunched over his plate and filled his mouth without knowing what it was he ate.

"What's wrong with you, boy?" his aunt asked.

But she was so full of excitement herself, that she didn't even wait for him to answer. And his uncle was excited too. He smiled and was dressed up in his Sunday suit and wore gold cuff links that he wore only on special occasions. At first Johnny thought his uncle was drunk but there was no smell of beer like there usually was when he had been drinking. Their excitement over the festival made him feel even more separate and lonely. Once he thought he was going to cry right there at the table.

"Something tells me I should have made three more pans of gingercake," Mary was saying. "Something tells me I should have made more."

"Smitty down at the bus terminal tells me there's going to be special trucks coming in from Munstor and Radcliffe," David said.

Johnny wondered why his uncle was so happy. Except for when his uncle was drunk, Johnny had never seen him in such high spirits before.

While they were eating their dessert of gingercake crumbs and cream, someone knocked at the door. Without knowing why, Johnny stopped breathing.

His aunt got up to answer the door.

"It's Baby Boy," she called from the doorway. "He wants you, Johnny."

He tried to keep from running but so great was his excitement, he almost knocked his aunt down at the kitchen doorway.

"Hi there, Baby Boy," Johnny said. He was very glad to see Baby Boy and he could hardly speak. "Come on in the parlor," he invited.

He was very proud to be able to invite Baby Boy into the parlor; it was his first guest in the three weeks he had been in Beetlecreek. Baby Boy was dressed in his Sunday suit and his hair was brushed. His face was very solemn.

Baby Boy didn't answer him or make any move to enter the house. Instead, he held out an envelope for Johnny to take and, as soon as it was in Johnny's hands, Baby Boy ran down the steps.

With hands trembling, Johnny ripped open the envelope. At first he thought that it was written in blood, but when he held it up to his nose he knew it was tomato catsup.

BE AT THE JUNK YARD AT TEN FIFTEEN PM OR YOUR NAME IS MUD—THE NIGHTRIDERS ! ! !

This was it, then. He would be initiated tonight. His first feeling was that of cold, numbing fear. What would they do to him? Across his mind flashed pictures of tortures he had seen in his history book, Indians holding burning torches to the chests of their victims, and people in England being stretched by ropes that pulled on their arms and legs in opposite directions.

Would he be able to stand such tortures or would he cry out for them to release him? Maybe he should hurry and tell them that he changed his mind and no longer wanted to be a member of the gang. But how could he? He would die of shame. He would have to go through with it.

His mouth became dry and every tendon in his legs and arms became as if charged with electricity. His jaws felt as if dry ice were on his teeth, and he vibrated all over as if a dentist's drill were in his mouth. He ate the rest of his cake, chewing it vigorously, as if to stop the dentist-drill feeling.

As soon as he could, he left the table and went upstairs to his room. During the half hour he lay there, all kinds of tortures came to his mind.

He used to pass time by imagining what he would do if suddenly he had to jump out of an airplane with a parachute. He would create each stage of the feeling until he had hypnotized himself with the idea of getting ready to jump. His stomach would feel hard as stone and his legs would become cold. Then he would stop breathing and begin to shake all over from the exertion.

Other times he would do the same thing until he had hypnotized himself into thinking he was about to be thrust into a roaring fire.

Once when he was very young, he fell off the porch and broke his leg. For a long time before anyone came to him, he lay on the ground delirious with the worst pain he had ever experienced. At the time, he thought that there could be no worse pain in all the world than that. He wondered if the pain of the initiation would be as great.

Later, while helping his aunt carry the gingercake pans to the church grass, he could hardly walk, so drugged was he from thinking about the initiation.

He left her as soon as he put down the pans, paying no attention to the activity that was transforming the church grass.

It was still early. He had more than two hours before time to meet the gang. He went to Telrico's where there were strangers hanging around, waiting for the festival to start.

A big group was around the pinball machine watching Wilson try to ring up twenty thousand on the red. Johnny stood on the fringe of the crowd and watched too. He noticed how graceful was the pulling back of the plunger and how gently the green carpeted sides and the rubber fences around the lights were bumped by the ball. More than ever, he felt apart from all the crowds and centers of excitement.

He perched himself on a stool and drank a bottle of Nehi, taking long, dawdling sips and looking down the straw into the bottle. Sometimes he would blow the brown pop back into the bottle to make bubbles.

A girl sat down beside him. She was pretty and had long brown hair. Johnny thought she looked like an Indian princess. He had never seen her before so she must have come into town that evening for the festival. From the corner of his eye, he could see her looking at him. She must have been fourteen or fifteen because she had big bubbies and wore thick pasty lipstick on her lips. She wore a black sateen dress that was very short so that Johnny could see a knee and part of her thigh.

She was looking at him frankly now and he began to drink his pop without fooling around.

"You from here?" she asked. Her voice was low and thin, like a skinny preacher's voice.

He turned around so that his body faced her, but he kept his head lowered to the pop bottle. He was very excited and felt a buzzing on his knees.

"No. I'm from Pittsburgh." He finished his pop with a loud sip and then lay the bottle on the counter so he could run his fingers over the frosted sides.

She kept on looking at him, at the same time, moving so close he could feel her knee touching the edge of his trousers.

"You sure are a long way from home," she said.

When he got up, she squeezed his knee slyly. "I hopes we see more of each other, sugarfoot," she said. "I'll be here all evening for the festival."

Johnny turned toward her briefly and tried to smile. Outside, he thought, I'll be able to see her after the initiation. After the initiation it would be all right to meet a girl. After the initiation, he knew he would know what to say to her and how to act. Now he was feeling too crazy. All he could do now was giggle and smile like a goop. Her voice was very sweet. She looked like an Indian princess.

It was quarter to nine. He could hear the loudspeaker being tested over at the church grass. Light was spilling out from the side of the church. It seemed as if everyone in the village were at the festival and as if all who weren't walked there as fast as they could go. The village was quiet and deserted. He walked in the very middle of the street. There were hardly any lights on in any of the houses. His fear remembered itself and became associated with the tight stillness.

He stopped at the side of the creek. He took down his trousers and stooped so that it fell with a frog splash into the water. The grass was cool and ticklish. He scooped his hand into the black mud near the water and squeezed it through his fingers. Later, he washed his hands, drying them on the big leaves of an oak sprout.

The water and creekside smelled like rotten flowers in the damp.

He knew that in a few more minutes it would be time for him to go but he knew they would be long minutes.

He thought of the first time he and his uncle were at Bill Trapp's house, how he had been caught by the old man while climbing up the apple tree and of how that fright was like what he was feeling now.

While buttoning up his trousers, he thought of the Indian princess and remembered how she squeezed his knee. He would go look for her as soon as he had been initiated. They would walk along the creek road in the dark and he would hold her hand, and with her sweet voice, she would ask him about himself, and he would tell her, very nonchalantly, that he had just been initiated by the Nightriders, a secret organization. And later they would go to Telrico's and sit in a booth together like the grownups do and he wouldn't care who saw them.

The junk yard was completely dark. Johnny walked rapidly through the bushes, holding his hand before him like a sleepwalker so that he wouldn't tear his new trousers on the thorns. As soon as he was in the clearing where slight moonlight gray gave depth to obscure objects around him, he stopped breathing and strained his ears to hear some reassuring sound. His heart was pounding and the rustle of the new corduroy when his legs brushed together kept him from identifying any close sound. Once he thought he heard a whirring noise but when he closed his eyes, he knew that it was only a cricket.

He went over to the derrick and sat on one of the planks. Maybe they had forgotten about the initiation and had gone to the festival instead. Maybe Baby Boy had been playing a prank on him. This idea swelled up inside him and the more he thought about it, the more likely it seemed. More minutes passed. He amused himself by feeling his pulse. He counted with the beats up to fifty and couldn't hear the footsteps approaching.

Suddenly, there they were in front of him. There were at least seven of them, all dressed in black robes, wearing black bags over their heads with holes cut for the eyes.

Johnny felt that he should say something but it was im-

159

possible for him to move his tongue. He could tell by the way they were standing and by the height of their silhouettes which was Baby Boy and which was the Leader. But the others he didn't know. The Nightriders must be a big club, he thought.

The Leader took him by the hand and, as if in a dream, Johnny rose to follow him. One of them tied a bandage over his eyes so tight he could see a galaxy of shapes and colors.

He heard whispering. There seemed to be some discussion as to where he should be taken first. He heard someone whisper, Gant's Tomb.

Gant's Tomb, he knew, was the colored folks' burying ground on the side of the hill above the railroad tracks. That was where the torture would take place then!

He tried to feel with his feet as he walked. He knew by the side to side rolling and the smell of the creek, when they crossed the swinging bridge. He knew when they climbed the embankment to get up on the railroad tracks. He almost slipped and fell on the cinders. He and the Leader headed the procession, the others followed closely and silently. He could hear only their concerted breathing and the shuffling of their feet.

Finally, they arrived at Gant's Tomb. He had never been there before, but had seen its tumbling white headstones and splintered rose trellis entrance from a distance.

He imagined smelling a strange odor in the cemetery, a smell like opening a trunk inside which a piece of bread had become moldy. He could hear the faint tinkling of the festival blown up the hillside from the village in the valley. The wind pulled at his bandage. He could hear a freight engine switching tracks at the roundhouse in Munstor.

They stopped and he was pushed down on a cool stone shape which he imagined to be a fallen tombstone.

"Gather round, brother Nightriders," said the Leader's voice. "Read the orders, brother secretary!"

A voice which Johnny didn't recognize began to read with mock seriousness, "Johnny Diggs, you is charged with secrecy of the initiation ceremony which is to follow."

Another voice, very high indeed, sounding very much like Baby Boy talking through a handkerchief muffler, said, "Do you swears on your life blood to keep all which will happen secret?"

Someone prodded Johnny. "Answer him!"

160

"I do," Johnny said, his voice choking on the words. If he could only control his breathing. If the air would only go out his nose instead of his mouth.

The Leader began speaking again. "The nightriders is a man's society and we don't want no kids foolin around. Now if you's ascared and don't want to join up, say so now or forever hold your peace."

"I want to belong," Johnny mumbled fervently.

"Well, all right then. We're going to give you a chance to be a man. The Nightriders's all men and each one of us has proved it by some courageous deed. You don't get into the club until you've proved to us you's a man."

What would they make him do? Johnny wondered. Would they make him stay out all night on some mysterious mission like they did to college students in a book he read once? He was no longer afraid of being tortured. Whatever they make me do, he told himself, I'll not be afraid. I'll prove to them that I'm a man and that I can take it. He felt like the new Johnny again. He smiled to himself as his fright left him. He bit his lower lip as if to prove to himself that he could stand pain.

He thought of the Indian princess and of the lipstick smile she gave him. He thought of being with her after the initiation, knowing that he would be a Nightrider—a man! And maybe they would see him in Telrico's with her. He would nod to them and smile, saying, "Hi, brothers, I want you to meet my girl friend."

They took his bandage off and sat on the ground in front of him. Only the Leader stood. It was too dark and he couldn't see the faces of the others.

"Are you ready to be charged with your duty?" the Leader asked. His voice was high and cracking as he tried to speak formally and slower than he usually spoke.

"Yes, sir," Johnny said. And he meant it. He tried to look straight into the Leader's eyes to show that he meant what he said. This was solemn. This was religious.

"We're goin with you, and if you try any monkey business, you don't get into the club, and you might get knocked around a bit, see?"

"You don't have to worry about me."

Johnny was anxious to know what he would have to do. He wanted to get it over with but, also, he was anxious to test

161

the new Johnny. There was nothing he feared. There was nothing they could propose to him that he wouldn't do. He'd show them he was a man worthy of their trust in him.

"Stand up!" the Leader ordered. And all the Nightriders stood up. "Give the sign!" he ordered. And they made a circle around Johnny and held each other's hands, at the same time mumbling something which Johnny couldn't understand.

"Raise yo right hand!"

Quivering with excitement and anxiety, Johnny raised his hand. Seconds seemed long and high as he waited for the Leader to speak.

"All right then. You knows this old white man Bill Trapp? You ought to know him—you used to hang out with him all the time."

There was a whisper of laughter around the circle.

"You knows all about what he did to those little Tolley girls. You knows how everybody talkin and ain't nobody doin nothing. Nightriders don't go in for all that talkin stuff. What we believe in is action. Ain't no peckerwood goin get away with that kind of stuff while we Nightriders's around. Everybody know what would of happened if it had been a colored man did all that funny stuff. Everybody knows, ain't nobody doin nothing about it. The Nightriders want action! To test whether you worthy of 'comin a member of the Nightriders, we hereby charges you to go out to Bill Trapp's shanty and burn it to the ground! Bring forth the gasoline!"

Cutting through the bushes below the railroad track, Johnny could hear the tramp, tramp, tramp of their footsteps behind him. None of them would speak; he refused to think. Before he knew it, he was across the swinging bridge. He walked as if he were in a dream. His steps seemed light and he couldn't tell when he put his feet down. Soon they were passing the bend in the creek—then the stone wall of the May Farm. Inside was Bill Trapp's shanty!

The gasoline cans, two of them, were cutting into the palm of his hand, but he hardly felt the weight of them. The Nightriders behind him tramped along noisily in single file, occasionally stumbling over their own robes. Under a street light he looked back to see the straggling line of black ghosts.

He was calm, too calm. It seemed as if he moved without any life inside him. He was only movement, no inner sensa-

BEETLECREEK

tion or substance. He felt like a ghost figure, too. Trees and bushes moved past him as if they were moving and not him. He could hear no sounds from the village. There were no dogs.

Just as he had done that first time when he was with the boys stealing apples from Bill Trapp, he crawled under the stone fence through a hole near a clump of bushes. The earth was wet and slimy. He didn't care about dirtying his Sunday clothes. He dragged the cans in after him. The others joined him on the other side.

"You got any matches?" the Leader asked.

Johnny shook his head. A box was located and shoved into his hands. It was much too dark to see, but he knew exactly where the house was. He could see the chimney standing alone against the sky above the hill. Baby Boy patted him on the shoulder; it was the only sensation he remembered. Then he ran across the grass.

He ran lightly as if he were being pushed by a gentle force behind him or as if he were sliding down a bannister to the house. In a moment he was there.

They had told him to pour the gasoline on a rolled up mat that was under the porch. They said it would catch quick because the logs of the house had been pitched with tar.

The mat was there and he poured the cool gasoline on it. His movements were smooth and efficient. The second can he poured on a pile of trash wood nearby and some he poured on the side of the shack.

Slowly and deliberately he took the matchbox and opened it. For only a moment he waited until the match flowered into a bulb of fire. Then he threw it in a slow falling arc on the bundled up mat.

It smoldered a moment, and then made a blue orange burst of light, like an automobile headlight suddenly appeared from around a curve. He was blinded and he smelled hair burning. He rubbed his eyebrows and discovered they had been singed by the burst of flame.

Slowly, he turned around and began to walk back to where the Nightriders waited. Then he ran. He began to laugh hysterically and stumbled over the shadow that became longer and longer in front of him as the fire grew.

He arrived at the tree where the others were waiting but they had disappeared. He could hear their footsteps pounding

163

on the road outside the wall. He was still laughing hysterically. He couldn't find the hole in the wall. He retraced his steps.

Only then did his movements stop gliding. Blood began moving inside him and he was no longer a ghost of movement. He seemed to wake. He looked, both fascinated and horrified, at the roaring flames. One whole side of the shanty was already burning and the field was lit as if in a fireworks display.

At first, he couldn't associate himself with the fire but then he realized he was still holding a gasoline can in his hand. As soon as he got outside the fence, he would throw it away.

He thought about the Indian princess, suddenly realizing that he must run away, far away, must escape, must escape. He had committed a terrible crime and he must escape.

He was sick and he stooped over to see if he could vomit. But no liquid came from his dry throat.

Without realizing what he was doing, he ran to the flaming house yelling, "Help, Help! Mr. Trapp! Mr. Trapp! Your house is on fire! Help! Help!"

But he could get no closer than fifteen yards to the house. He's burning to death in there, Johnny thought. He imagined seeing the old man's kindly face surrounded by flames.

He scratched his face. He jumped up and down. He blew out of the corner of his mouth. He wet his pants.

He must get away! He had murdered a man. Bill Trapp was burning to death. There was a rhythmic crackling to the fire. Johnny imagined he heard a soft, almost inaudible groaning over the crackling.

He ran completely around the shanty twice; ran as if he were in a race, fast, lifting his knees high, digging his toes in the sod. Then he ran to the stone fence. He must get away! He must get away! Why had he ever agreed to do such a thing?

At the stone fence, he still couldn't find the hole. He ran from bush to bush. He fell over the stump of a tree into a hole covered by vines. He felt as if he were trapped, and fought and fought, thrashing his arms about like a madman.

On his feet once more, he ran from one dark shadowy place to the other, finding no hole. He ran along the stone wall taking tiny frantic steps. Suddenly, he straightened up and stopped dead in his tracks. There, standing beside him, holding onto the trunk of the tree, his features exaggerated by the light from the fire, stood Bill Trapp. On his face was a sad, resigned look.

"What have you done, Johnny?" was all he said. He put out his hand and touched Johnny's shoulder.

When Johnny felt the old man's hand on him, he began to shake with terror and rage. The old man grabbed him and hugged him close.

"What have you done, Johnny? What have you been up to?"

There was a blinding light inside him, a blinding light that lit him up inside from his stomach to his head, a blinding green streak of lightning. Outside this inside light, he could feel the old man's hands on him. He felt as if his blood had been changed into hot steel. He must get away! He must get away!

His fist closed tighter on the handle of the gasoline can and he felt his arm swinging out in a high swooping arc. And he heard a dull clang. And he felt Bill Trapp become limp. And he saw him fall to the ground.

Johnny ran and ran through the trees. He followed a path lit by the flames. He climbed a tree and swung over the wall. He jumped. He realized he was hurt and bleeding. He ran and ran and ran.

He heard the train switching in Munstor.

He heard fire engines.

■ CHAPTER TWO

THERE were many moths about, all of them fuzzy and made of gray-brown powder. In and out of the shadows they flitted, between lanterns and under the booths, appearing momentarily in patches of light, casting bat shadows on the ground. One of them flew in Mary's pan of gingercake.

"My goodness, these moths!" she exclaimed, as if talking to someone beside her. But she was all alone. Johnny, who had helped her carry the heavy pans to the church grass, had seemed preoccupied and left as soon as he set the pans down in her booth.

The church grass was decorated with banners and strips of colored crepe paper. A sagging string of lights which stretched from the corner of the church to a nearby telephone pole, illuminated the line of booths. Several of the booths, especially one which bore a long FISH POND sign, had real jack o'lanterns with candles in them for lights. The church grass was high and uncut around the booths, but in a short while, there would be paths around them, beat down by the crowds.

Mary looked at her signs with approval. Her booth was right in the center of the best lighted area, and the red, green, and gold shone like the sides of a circus wagon.

Smiling happily to herself, she walked a few steps away from the booth to examine it from all possible angles. Then she sidled up to it as if she were a customer and leaned on the counter.

"What you doin there, leanin on the counter day dreamin like that, gal?" Helen Perkins and Sally Dunn had slipped up behind her. Each was carrying the handle of a huge wash hamper.

"Just thought I'd come early," she replied. "Takes time to set up a pretty booth like mine's goin to be."

"Well, you sure has a nice one, honey," Sally Dunn said admiringly.

"Way I hear it," Helen Perkins said, mopping her brow with a man's bandanna, "we're set to have a record attendance. Big bunch from Brady Mine expected on the eight-thirty car, another bunch comin all the way up from Bradford, makin a hay ride out of it with three or four trucks."

"Yes. I certainly hopes we has a nice crowd this year. We certainly worked hard enough."

"We sure did, honey. We sure did."

"What time is it?" asked Helen Perkins.

"Goin on quarter to eight," Mary said, looking at the Mickey Mouse watch she had borrowed from the youngest Pinkerton girl for the occasion.

"Well, better hurry up and get set up. Crowds start flocking in here before you know it."

It was becoming gradually darker now and down by the swinging bridge there was no remnant of sunset light in the sky. Other ladies arrived, and with them little children who began hanging around the booths, their eyes big, looking hungrily at the bestest gingercake, asking in eager mouth-organ voices if there was anything they could do to help.

Finally, Mrs. Tolley arrived. And with her were the two little girls, Mary Ellen and Sarah, who clung very tightly to their mother's hands, who kept their eyes lowered to the grass.

It was the very first time Mary had seen Mrs. Tolley since the tragedy and she realized with a quick tug of triumph, that there was something beat down and defeated about the fat woman's walk. It's all been very hard on her, poor soul, Mary thought. But teasing in the back of her mind, was the thought that Mrs. Tolley's seven unchallenged years of presidency were coming to an end. Her heart beat faster when she thought of the last meeting when she had been chairman.

Looking at the two little girls, both of whom were dressed identically in red coats and tams, a shade of sadness passed over her, for she could have no children of her own. But this feeling quickly passed because she was being swept along by the growing flood of festival excitement. This is a special night in the world, she thought, a night for her, a special night full of special secret meanings.

Mrs. Tolley called the ladies to the center of the church grass. Mary waited a long time before she would join them.

She finished folding the napkins Mrs. Pinkerton had given her and made sure her frilled apron was on straight. When she joined the ring of ladies standing around Mrs. Tolley's Fish Pond, she heard her saying: ". . . and girls that means that each and every one of us has to put special effort into our selling this year. . . ."

But Mary thought Mrs. Tolley wasn't speaking at all with the fire and spirit the occasion warranted. Mrs. Tolley wasn't the same since the tragedy! Mrs. Tolley wasn't acting at all like a president should act just before an important festival!

Before Mary realized just what she was doing, she had walked to Mrs. Tolley's side. The festival excitement inside her pushed her on.

"And that ain't all, girls," she heard herself saying. "We've *got* to get the money these folks bringing into town tonight! The church *needs* it, the Missionary Guild *needs* it, and we've got to *get* it!"

She felt choked up inside her and could say no more, but what she had said was said with such throaty earnestness, that when she had finished, there was for a moment complete silence. But only for a moment, because then they began applauding her and cheering her—even Mrs. Tolley—and she felt them pounding her on the back.

She went back to her booth, the ladies' congratulations in her ears.

Then the main lights were turned on: red, blue, and yellow lights strung in a criss-cross pattern down the main walk between the booths. Mary stood at her counter, filled with happy, childlike anticipation. This was a special night! A wonderful, happy special night!

All around her was soft laughter and whooping of small children hanging around the booths. More and more moths appeared around the aura of light at each booth and dogs that followed the children began running around in circles behind the church.

The sky became darker, remoter, until the church grass was the whole world and became a round festival place. Each booth became a glittering palace presided over by a proud, smiling queen. The church bell rang.

By eight-thirty, Mary had already sold several pieces of gingercake, one of them to the Reverend himself. In twos and

168

threes, people began coming until the church grass was crowded.

A loud-speaker system was being tried out. It had arrived late from Bell Electric uptown. Children crowded around the truck as the metallic monotony of, Testing, one two . . . swung over the grounds. Presently, a gay fast-step filled the air with music. It was an old song, "Tiptoe Through the Tulips," played as if it were a hill-billy song, but it didn't matter, there were no jazz records uptown. The rented speaker system was electric and magic, and children watched with mouths agape as the turntable played rasping melodies, one after the other.

At first, Mary busied herself cutting the gingercake into equal squares. She would dig the end of the knife ever so gently into the soft cake and then bear down until the knife made a jangly, scraping sound as it dragged the bottom.

Then, all at once, she was besieged by customers. Most of them were hungry, marble-eyed children, spending their first nickels on the famous gingercake. But once, one of the white men from Bell Electric bought a piece of cake and lingered at the counter to talk to her.

"Sure is good cake, ma'am," he said, friendly like, addressing her in the twanging accents of the nearby mountains.

Mary felt a shiver of pride partly because of the compliment, but also because he said, "ma'am."

She smiled down at the counter as she took his nickel, saying, "Well, ain't nearly as good as it should be, what with the depression and all, but we try to do our best."

There wasn't much space in Mary's booth, but there was a great crystal palace feeling because of the light from the 100-watt lamp in the pumpkin that reflected on the white tablecloth and enameled pans. The light shone on the grass, too, and under the counter so that she could look at the reflection of the rhinestones on the buckles of her shoes.

She felt festive and gay. She felt like the ladies who came to Mrs. Pinkerton's for tea and bridge parties, like the ladies who stood behind the bottle jewels at the perfume counter in King's department store downtown. She identified herself with all the ladies of the world: the tennis champions, the pilots, the debutantes, the cheerleaders, the models, the movie stars, the New York women, the girls in the *True Romance*. . . . Tonight she belonged! She was one of them.

She smiled on everyone who came to her booth, she flirted

with Mr. Anderson and the Reverend, she shouted at the other ladies and echoed their hawking cries, shrilling out in a thin voice, "H'yare! Mary's Bestest Gingercake! Better get it while it's hot! Get it while it's hot!" Then, she would break out in a laugh that would make everybody within hearing distance laugh too.

The music blared out "Tiptoe Through the Tulips," over and over again, and a rasping joking voice urged the customers to have their fortunes told.

The Reverend was everywhere. He came over to Mary's booth for the third time, dressed in his picnic suit of gray flannel with broad green stripes and a yellow shirt, smiling, wiggling his ears, leaning on the counter and drumming his cross against the wooden crosspiece.

"You certainly have the gift of the angels when it comes to making the most wonderful gingercake I have had the pleasure of tasting," he said. And it sounded as if he were praying. But Mary was delighted and urged him to have the third piece free which he didn't refuse, excusing himself for just a moment to go to the next booth to fetch a glass of lemonade to drink with it. He came back wiping the crumbs from his mouth, his lips reflecting the light on the greasy slime.

"You have served the Missionary Guild so faithfully," he said, "that I wouldn't be a bit surprised if you didn't get the nomination for presidency at the next regular meeting." He whispered confidentially, patting her hand and picking up a stray crumb of gingercake with a quick, bird snatch.

"It's most kind of you, Reverend, to talk to me like that but I don't have no ambitions in that line."

She could hardly give correct change, she was so happy. She was soaring. She was drunk. She felt stretched and loved by everything. She would have given free gingercake to all the hungry-eyed children leaning on the end of the counter but she must make as good a showing financially as she could.

Just like every happy experience she had ever had, everything that was happening now—the music coming over the loudspeaker, the general hum of laughing, screaming, jingling, jangling, whirring, and shuffling, the smell of her own gingercake, the smell of hotdogs and mustard and barbecue —seemed like an unreal dream.

Once, soon after she married David, they went sled riding

on the hill back of the railroad. They rode belly-down all the way to the bottom of the hill and it was wonderful. It was the only time in her whole life she had ever been sled riding, the only time, and it was wonderful and a dream-like thing. Often she would tell the youngest Pinkerton girl about that time sled riding. But Mary would say they roasted marshmallows and wieners before a huge fire and sang songs, which wasn't true. But it was Mary's habit to elaborate and reweave the incomplete happinesses of her life. She would smooth them and round them to make them conform with the ideals she formed by reading *Good Housekeeping* magazine and the *Ladies' Home Journal* which she would bring home from Pinkertons' and put on the table by her bed to read before falling asleep.

The nickels in Mary's cigar box began to pile up and she no longer had time to count them. When she had to make change, she would scoop her hand deep in the pile, reveling in the feeling of cold coins slipping through her fingers.

Mary had no time to think, only feel, and the festival around her, the crowds and countless strange faces that appeared momentarily before her were all part of the gay, merry-go-round dream. She was in a delirium of excitement and all the while the pile of nickels grew higher and higher.

She had no time even to think of what the Reverend had said. But about that, she didn't have to think. The idea was there in the rosiness of her mind. Here, at the festival, in the wondrous mystery that was all that was going on about her, in the drunkenness of the growing pile of nickels, in the lights, in the music coming over the loudspeaker, she could believe it. It *could* be true, her nomination as president. And it was this idea that was at the bottom of her happiness.

Quickly, she ran through one, two, three pans of gingercake. She could have sold three times as much as she brought. Truly it was the biggest crowd in the history of the festival.

She felt very sad when the last pan was almost emptied— sad, not because she could have sold more if she had made it, but sad because the wonderful merry-go-round dream feeling was coming to an end.

Now, there was a sudden rush of customers eager to buy the remaining pieces of gingercake and it was all she could do to handle the grasping fingers reaching across the counter toward her rapidly emptying pan. Finally it was empty and there were groans of disappointment. Then, the children, who all evening had stood restlessly at the end of her booth, suddenly came to life and surged under the counter.

She held them at bay, laughing and giggling till her eyes filled. This moment was her greatest pleasure. This was when she became boss lady, queen. She wanted to shout and shout and sing. If there had been a dance floor, she would have gone there to dance. She felt like a young girl at her first party, she felt like the Pinkerton girl looked when she came in, flushed with excitement, dressed in her white, cheerleader's sweater, from the football game. Her power was limitless and she knew she could be the president of the Missionary Guild, knew she could lead them on to bigger, better things.

"All right! All right!" she shouted at the children, leaping up and down like hounds under her raised arms. "Don't you all fight now or I ain't going to give nobody none of these crumbs." And her voice had new command to it.

They stood quietly while she gathered the crumbs and bits of gingercake and placed them in equal quantities in neatly folded napkins, one for each child. Then, when all was quiet, she swept up the scraps of paper, gathered the borrowed pans, and made ready to close her booth.

Now, the church grass was almost deserted. The lights in some of the booths had already been turned off and already the children of some of the ladies paraded around the lot with jack o'lanterns, getting ready to cart them home. Some of the ladies were gathered around the lemonade stand, drinking what was left of the lemonade and eating cold hotdogs rolled up in slices of white bread.

The two white men from Bell Electric uptown were taking down the wires of the loud-speaker system. One of them spoke to Mary while he unfastened the wires attached to her booth.

"You all sure had a crowd here tonight," he said.

Mary was counting her nickels, dropping them one by one into a twenty-five pound sugar sack. She was counting out loud and could only nod her head and smile in way of reply.

"Yessir," she said finally. "We had a pretty good bunch of folks."

The man from Bell Electric had taken down the wire and was still standing in front of the booth.

"That old white man that lives out here about somewheres —whatever become of him?"

A sharp, warning feeling, a dark green shape, came from the back of her mind to spoil the rosy happiness. Somewhere, something was wrong. Something was going to happen. Mention of the old man made her think of Johnny and her husband. Where were they? Both had said they would be along later, but she had seen neither of them.

"Well, now, he lives around here all right," she said, "but I ain't seen him. Ain't nobody seen him lately and the way they talkin around, it's a good thing." Her voice was tinged with anger, because now she associated Bill Trapp with this threat to her happiness, and attributed to him the absence of her nephew and husband. Somehow he had kept them from witnessing her moments of triumph.

"Funny old bird to do a thing like that, heard about it down at the American Legion . . . oh well . . . just goes to show it takes all kinds. . . ."

As soon as the man left her, Mary joined the other ladies already gathered around Mrs. Tolley's Fish Pond. Mrs. Tolley was dipping water out of her fish pond looking for the grand prize fish which no one had won. Mary noted with great satisfaction that only about half the prizes had been won, that Mrs. Tolley's Fish Pond had not been a success.

"I didn't expect nobody to win the grand prize, not the way I had number thirteen fish hid," Mrs. Tolley gloated, pulling the tin fish out of a crack in the corner of the pond. She winked at the ladies.

"Whoo-ee! We sure made good tonight!" Helen Perkins shouted, swinging her bag of coins over her head.

"Yes, indeed, ladies. You all have certainly done very well for yourselves. Now if you'll just come inside the church to my office, we'll get ready for the general accounting." The Reverend's eyes were shining and he leaned over the counter very close to the moneybags. His smile took in each of the ladies in turn and he smiled at the moneybags.

Mary, clutching tight to her sugar sack, felt her warning fears disappear as she anticipated the moment when she would make her report in front of all the ladies.

She went back to her booth to gather up all the pots and pans, deciding that she would leave them in the church till the next day when Johnny could help her with them.

The red, blue, and yellow lights were turned off and the church grass came to darkness again. The children left, the dogs left, and with no more light to attract them, the moths.

With darkness, seemingly, came complete silence. Mary was all alone in the middle of the church grass. Her crystal palace was no more for that year, but she had memories and impressions enough to last her for a long time. And, most important of all, the Reverend himself had complimented her, had hinted to her of nomination for the presidency of the guild.

The next day, when the Pinkerton girl would come into the kitchen after school for milk and graham crackers, she would tell her about the festival. She would tell her how she emptied three whole pans of gingercake way before the festival was over, and she would tell her about the genuine lighting effects and the loudspeaker that played dance music all evening.

The other ladies had already entered the church. Mary was all alone in the middle of the church grass and she felt that she should pray. If she knew what it was she wanted, she would have. If she knew what was the unspoken longing that filled her sometimes walking home through the shady lanes of the pink-roofed part of town, or at one of Mrs. Pinkerton's tea parties while she served the relaxed, fan-waving ladies in tea dresses and wide hats—if she knew for what this longing was, then and there she would have prayed for it. But, already that night, part of the longing had been fulfilled.

For a long time, she stood in front of her booth enchanted by the skeleton frames of the booths in the darkness and the melancholy feeling of being the last one to leave the church grass. The crepe-paper decorations no longer had color to them but waved back and forth with the breeze that had come as soon as the festival was over.

There was a cool, unpleasant dampness in the air and she felt chilly. The freak summer was coming to an end.

She gathered up her pans, her sack of money, and her memories and left the church grass, walking very slowly, dragging her feet over the beat down grass, humming very softly to herself, "Tiptoe Through the Tulips. . . ."

■ CHAPTER THREE

ONLY a handful of people were waiting for the eleven-fifteen northbound to arrive from Munstor. Most of them were hillbillies riding as far as Tulip where they would take the shuttle bus to National Park. David thought they looked pitifully ill at ease standing motionless and open mouthed in the very middle of the floor inside the flashy blue and nickel bus station.

He straightened his tie and pulled down the back of his blue suit jacket and walked boldly past them, feeling very smug and contented, knowing he had a long strip of yellow ticket with full insurance in his pocket, knowing he would ride through the night, straight into Pittsburgh (forty minute layover), straight to Cleveland (hour and a half rest stop), all the way to Detroit.

He had a five-cent raisin pie in his pocket which he wanted to eat. He was hungry, but he wouldn't eat it in front of the hillbillies. He would go to the entrance of the washroom and eat it. Afterwards, maybe, he would get a shoeshine.

He looked at his watch. It was already eleven-one. He hoped the watch would keep running until he arrived in Pittsburgh. While riding in a dark, enclosed bus, he was nervous if every ten minutes he didn't know the exact time.

There were no Negroes hanging around the bus station. Apparently they had all gone to the church festival, all except Doc who substituted shining shoes for Mr. Morgan on Saturday nights. Doc wasn't right in the head.

"Howdeedo, Mr. Diggs. Put yo feet heah in my lap an let me polish them off. . . . Dreamed bout a gold mouse last night, Mr. Diggs. Play seven seven seven soon's yo get to Pittsburgh."

"I'm going all the way to Detroit, Doc."

"Play seven seven seven soon's yo get to Detroit. . . ."

David looked with pleasure at his new blue silk socks and at the fine gloss the new tan shoes were taking. Nothing like a good shine to give a man that final touch, he said to himself, remembering an advertisement he had seen once.

He looked at his watch again. Eleven-five. Why doesn't the girl come?

"Gold mouse was in ordinary trap, wooden trap. Had a been gold trap and wooden mouse, woulda been seven seven six, but it was gold mouse all right, saw it just as plain as I sees these shoes."

"I'll play seven seven seven soon's I get to Detroit."

Poor Doc, he thought, I'll give him a fifteen-cent tip. David didn't have much money—enough to last a week or so in the city—but he wouldn't begin economizing now.

He wondered what his wife would say when she read the note: Going to Detroit for a week, will write as soon as I arrive. She'd be surprised all right. She'd say, Lord have mercy, he's left. And run to all the neighbors crying. And Johnny would look at the note and wouldn't say anything.

How strange that he didn't feel any remorse, any guilt, about leaving this way. All evening he'd been so excited that he was hardly able to pack a suitcase. But then, they'd been excited too, excited about the festival. They can have all that church foolishness, he mumbled, I'm going to Detroit; now where *is* that girl?

"Bring me a souvenir back from Detroit, Mr. Diggs."

You poor bastard, Doc, he thought, you poor carbon-faced bastard with your yellow stumps and pink-patched gums. . . .

"They got toy autos filled with candy, Mr. Diggs . . . bring me a souvenir?"

"Sure thing, Doc. Don't worry, I'll bring you something back."

"Don't forget to play seven seven seven *soon's* you put yo feet on land . . . seven seven seven."

One of the hillbillies, a tall bucktoothed youth wearing a cowboy hat and a baby-blue silk shirt, came into the washroom.

"How soon yaa-all finished, Doc?" the hillbilly asked.

Those hillbillies all talk like they've got a mouthful of guitars, David thought.

"Finished right away, sir. Right away. Yes, sir . . . finished

. . . right . . . away . . . fin . . . ished . . . right . . . a
. . . way . . . right . . . A . . . WAY. . . . There y'are, Mr.
Diggs. . . . THANK YOU, Mr. Diggs! . . . Now you step right up
there, sir. . . ."

David walked out of the washroom and went to the news-
stand. He chose a *Readers' Digest* to read on the bus. He
glanced contemptuously at one of the hillbilly ladies who was
choosing a *Red Star Comics*.

"Give me a giant Hershey, too," he said.

Again he looked at his watch. Then he walked over to
where he could see the official Western Electric time in the
dispatcher's office. Eleven-nine.

NORTHBOUND FROM CINCINNATI AND MUNSTOR
LEAVING AT GATE NUMBER ONE FOR PITTSBURGH
BUFFALO AND ALL POINTS NORTH. . . .

This was his bus! Where *is* that girl?

He ran to the street and looked up and down. She was
nowhere to be seen. She'd probably come at the last minute
in a taxi. David decided he better get aboard and claim a
good seat. The bus seemed to be crowded.

The bus looked to be high as a ship. He was conscious of
sleepy white faces looking down at him from the nickel
framed windows.

"Have your tickets ready."

Scanning the row of windows, David noticed immediately
a black face in the rear window looking at him.

David unfolded his ticket so that the length of it flapped
in the breeze. The hillbillies looked at the ticket. David stood
aside to let them enter first, but they wouldn't enter before
him.

Pittsburgh-Detroit. Clip-clip. Step up. Move lively now.

The inside of the bus was like a movie theater. David
walked stiffly, bumping his suitcase against the sides of the
seats. Stony sleepy white faces looked into his eyes as he
passed. He smelled sweat, but it wasn't him. He'd just had a
bath. He saw an empty seat near the front. He thought, I
could sit there if I wanted to, they've got the new law. He
saw the black face looking at him from the back seat. The
entire back was empty. He could sleep back there. The
colored man was making room for him.

David moved through the white faces on either side of him all the way to the back. He put his suitcase on the rack and took off his hat, placing it in the middle of the cushion. Then he unfastened his tie.

He looked at the colored man. Southern darkie, he thought, looks scared to death, probably going north to work.

A cat slipped in the doorway and walked down the aisle. Only he and the darkie could see it. The darkie rolled his eyes over to David and for a moment they communicated their secret information. Then he pretended he didn't see the cat.

The cat came back and rubbed his legs. The darkie rolled his eyes over to him again and they communicated. But still they didn't say anything. David wondered if he should pick the cat up and carry it off the bus; the cat couldn't make the whole trip. The bus driver would think that it was his.

The darkie was thinking the same thing, David thought, but he wasn't making any move to pick the cat up. What if the cat mee-oowed. People would all turn around and look at them; they'd think it belonged to the darkies. Maybe they'd giggle. The bus driver would come back and say something smart.

The bus driver started the motor.

God! He's leaving, David thought, rising out of his seat. No. The bus driver got up again and left the bus to enter the dispatcher's office.

The darkie reached down to pat the cat.

Good, David thought, it's all the darkie's responsibility now.

The bus became altogether quiet above the throbbing of the engine. The darkie put the cat on his lap, put his coat over it and stroked it under the coat.

The bus driver came out of the dispatcher's office.

Just when David was resigned to getting off the bus and going to look for the girl, a taxi drove up. It's her, he thought, filled with joy and relief. He leaned over the darkie and stuck his head out of the window. "Hurry up, Edith. You can get your ticket in here!"

Everybody was looking at him, but he didn't care. The darkie was looking at him with new interest.

Edith entered the bus. God, she's pretty, David thought.

178

She smiled at the bus driver and leaned her hips on him while she opened her purse.

The driver took her bag and carried it back to the seat David saved for her. David noticed with pride how all the white faces turned to look at the pretty big-city girl.

"Thank you very kind. . . ." Edith smiled at the bus driver again.

The bus driver roared the engine. R-rr-umm-umm.

People settled down in their seats, twisting and turning to find a position with which they could sleep. A hillbilly baby woke up and began crying. The darkie put both hands over the coat. He's going to keep the cat, David thought.

"I thought you weren't going to make it," David said, leaning close to Edith. She smelled like whiskey and beer.

"You're cute," she said, patting his cheek.

The bus pulled out of the station and twisted around the corner to Main Street. The bus crept along the street, honking its horn at the Saturday night traffic. The Salvation Army band struck up a march-hymn at the intersection while the bus waited for a red light. *Tarzan and the Green Death* was playing at the Ritz.

"What's eating you?" she asked. She lit a cigarette and handed him one.

"I'm finally making the trip," he said. "After all these years. . . ."

She laughed contemptuously. "You're cute," she said.

But he felt very strange inside about it all, felt strange because he didn't feel much of anything.

He remembered that he left the toilet flushing. What if it would fill up the bathroom. . . .

Me-ooow.

David looked to see if any of the white faces had turned around. But they couldn't hear because of the hillbilly baby's crying.

"What'll you do about the house?" he asked her.

"It's been mortgaged twice," she said. "Sell it for the principal. Home Loan'll take care of it, don't you worry . . . white bastards. . . ."

After a while she asked him, "Do you want a drink?"

Where does she get all the whiskey, he wondered. "Aahh. That's good."

"Hits the spot," she said.

He wondered if she would offer the darkie some. The darkie was rolling his eyes toward them, was scratching his head, was rubbing the cat.

The lights were turned off. David leaned over toward Edith and slipped his arms around her. She squirmed out of his grasp. "Don't always be so goddamned lovey-dovey," she said. Her voice was dry and scraping.

They were at the foot of Main Street, passing Ford Motors, Perkin's Music Store, Greenhill Florists, Baily Brothers' Undertakers.

"Want a piece of chocolate?" he asked her.

"No," she answered, "and don't go getting those crumbs all over the seat."

The bus stopped with a jerk. There were fire engines. The chief's car went by. A second fire engine passed. The siren was so loud and close that David didn't hear it until it turned the corner. Red lights seemed to be flashing everywhere.

The white faces woke up with a start. The darkie opened the window and stuck his head out. Edith leaned back and yawned. David was frightened. Fire engines always frightened him.

The cat walked off the darkie and walked onto David's lap.

Me-ooow.

"Nice cat," Edith said. "Here, kitty, kitty. . . . Wonder where it is—the fire?"

"I don't know," he answered. He thought, Whole goddamned town could burn down and I wouldn't give a damn, let's start the bus again, let's go, let's go; let's go over the mountain to Munstor, across the river to Uniontown, past Uniontown to Pittsburgh; let's go, let's go. . . .

"Stop squirming in your seat so," Edith said. "Where'd this cat come from? Is it yours?"

"No, ma'am," the darkie said. "That's my cat!"

The last fire engine had passed and the driver started the motor again.

AFTERWORD

AFTERWORD

When William Demby's novel *Beetlecreek* was originally published in 1950 it received good notices from some reviewers, who duly observed that it was a first novel by a promising young talent and hoped that the author would fulfill his potential in future work. It should be noted that *Beetlecreek* appeared before the widespread current interest in the writing of American Negroes. It was a first novel by a Negro writer who had neither a literary or public reputation and who was living abroad.

This story of a young Negro boy, Johnny, who arrives from Pittsburgh to live with his aunt and uncle in Beetlecreek, his involvement with a strange and lonely old white man and the effects of that involvement and its ultimate repudiation by the Negro community is, of course, a story that involves a certain tension between its Negro and white characters. However the territory of the novel encompasses a much broader area than racial conflict. The old white man, the uncle, and the young Negro boy are "outsiders." They seek acceptance by the community, but at the conclusion of the novel they remain defeated. The events in *Beetlecreek* occur in an atmosphere of spiritual and emotional vacuity where hope and desire lead only to hysteria, violence and tragedy.

Although *Beetlecreek* is a most compelling story, American readers were unprepared for a novel about Negroes and whites that was not concerned with "race relations," that was not a "protest novel" dealing with that issue Americans so fastidiously call civil rights. Instead, *Beetlecreek* belongs to that tradition of literature that questions the human condition, that is concerned with the interior meaning and reality of man's fate, of both Black Man and White Man. Demby does protest against the universal human condition for, as he tells us in a later work, "life is existence and existence is sacred."

Beetlecreek appeared two years before Ralph Ellison's brilliant *Invisible Man* and three years before *Go Tell It on the Mountain,* James Baldwin's first novel. In its concern with questions relating to alienation, identity, and in the use of "Negro" as a metaphor for all whose lives are denied dignity and meaning in modern society, Demby's book anticipated themes which were to significantly appear in the work of other writers after the publication of *Beetlecreek.*

With two exceptions, *Beetlecreek* received no serious critical attention and soon passed out of print and into oblivion until the Avon Library publication of this reprint edition. In his study *The Negro Novel in America,* published in 1958, Robert Bone discussed Demby's novel and wrote that *Beetlecreek:*

"is an existentialist novel whose central characters come momentarily to life only to return in the end to somnambulance. It is, moreover, an expatriate novel, whose tone is dominated by pessimism and disgust, flowing from a robust rejection of American culture and of Negro life in particular. Viewed psychologically, it is a novel of cramped desire . . ."

"Cramped desire" is indeed the major characteristic of those living in Beetlecreek. The author most effectively uses a group or barbershop cronies as a chorus to tell us about the hopelessness of this town and to suggest the inevitability of tragedy. In a sense, *Beetlecreek* is a novel that goes beyond the possibilities of an existentialism that affirms the right, even the necessity for the individual to make his own way, and to find his own truths. In the existentialist view the ultimate responsibility for man is man. The barbershop chorus conveys to the reader that this is a meaningless premise for those who live in a world that views independence as an act of betrayal, the world of *Beetlecreek.*

In 1963, for the firm of Alfred A. Knopf, I edited an anthology of contemporary Negro literature and included a section of *Beetlecreek.* In commenting on Demby's novel, I wrote that:

"*Beetlecreek* is a highly imaginative work, rich with symbolic meaning and suggestion and concerned with questions of good and evil that go beyond race.

"In this novel the complex relationship between individual white persons and colored persons is treated with an unusual sensitivity and the life of the Negro world is harshly and honestly depicted. In *Beetlecreek*, Negroes are as much the victims of one another as they are of white society.[1]

Re-reading the novel now, some years later, I am once again impressed with the honesty of the work. One senses that events happened because they had to happen. There is no intrusion of form for the sake of literary effect. Indeed, Demby has created a novel where the "literary effect" is an integral part of the work. His style does not separate out from his intent, and it is this that contributes to the novel's impact. Here is demonstrated the skill of a writer who knows how to let events proceed out of themselves, out of the confrontation of characters. It is this, finally, that sparks the novel's revelations.

In its telling of the terrors of a white man's life and of the philistinism and constriction of the Negro community of Beetlecreek, Demby describes the dilemma, and the frustration of unexamined fears, that confront both Negroes and whites.

William Demby was born in Pittsburgh in 1922 and spent his early youth in Clarksburg, West Virginia, a coal mining region which is the setting for *Beetlecreek*. In 1947 he graduated from Fisk University in Nashville, Tennessee. Since 1949 Mr. Demby has traveled abroad extensively and has worked as a writer and translator for the European motion picture and television industry. He has written screen treatments for Roberto Rosellini, the eminent Italian film director, but also does commercial "hack" work for popular television programs.

After an initial visit to Italy during his two years in the American Army, where he wrote for the Army newspaper *Stars and Stripes*, Demby returned to Rome to study painting and to work as a jazz musician (alto saxophone). He periodically returned to the United States for brief visits and during 1964 he worked as a writer in a New York advertising agency. Mr. Demby with his wife and son now makes his permanent home in Rome.

[1] Herbert Hill, ed., *Soon, One Morning: New Writing by American Negroes*, Alfred A. Knopf, N. Y., 1963. See also Herbert Hill, ed., *Anger and Beyond: The Negro Writer in the United States*, Harper and Row, N. Y. 1966.

In a recent private letter, Mr. Demby comments:

"I have always lived in Europe as an adult. I would prefer living in the United States, I think, if the social scientists would stop breaking we new American writers (new American writers to become) and let us think and put it down in words. The Negro problem is a not so clever diversion . . . if we are not alert and careful now in America we shall be woven into the very fabric of our myths."

His second novel, *The Catacombs,* was published in 196? and is set in Europe. In commenting on contemporary life i? both Europe and America, Demby writes: "Evils purge evils but when will the chain of evils end?" The characters in *Th? Catacombs,* like the fictional author in the novel, are ". . beginning to have the strangest feeling that we are all nothing more than shadows, spirits, breathed into life, and manipulated by Pirandello's fertile mind."

The Catacombs is a powerful and original work writter in an unusual cinematic style—the fast imposition of imag? over image—that reveals Demby's unique perspective and literary skill. He is now at work on a third novel entitled *The Long Bearded Journey.* He recently wrote that:

"The Catacombs is different from Beetlecreek and The Long Bearded Journey is different from The Catacombs. I shall never allow myself to become iceberged into a style. There is much I want to say and I am convinced that the American Negro experience is historically unique."

Demby's awareness of the uniqueness of the Negro experience in the United States, together with his private sense of modern man's estrangement from an absurd world, has created his special "angle of vision," his highly critical view of contemporary life. The dehumanization and brutalization of American society in its obsessive preoccupation with race and color must be understood as part of a larger process of social disintegration. In his writing Demby repeatedly refers to the theme of sickness and suggests that we have entered into a period of eclipse that is profound and shattering in its moral implications. In his later novel, he asks, ". . . why this long shadow over America? How long will this sickness last?"

In *Beetlecreek* Demby sharply and dramatically poses these questions as he tells the story of a white outsider in relation to a community of Negroes, who are also outsiders. In *Beetlecreek* the author has an uncloying, restrained sympathy for the outsider, white or colored, who suffers from the treatment of an insensitive and malicious society, a cruel society that consists of Negroes as well as whites. To have written a novel such as *Beetlecreek*, whatever its limitations, is to have achieved a great deal.

While still a student in a creative writing class at Fisk University, Demby wrote several short stories for the *Fisk Herald*, the student publication. As assistant editor of the magazine, he frequently drew illustrations and contributed reviews and articles. In the *Fisk Herald* of December, 1946, Demby's short story, "Saint Joey" appeared. This story, used later in a much-altered form, contained the original basis for the novel *Beetlecreek*.

In "Saint Joey" Demby told of a gang of white adolescents who decide to murder an aging recluse because he has, in his own private manner, violated what the white gang regards as the established pattern of Negro-white relations. In *Beetlecreek* this idea is significantly transformed as the gang now consists of Negro boys engaged in the destruction of an old white man who seeks to end his long isolation from the world by establishing contact with the Negro community. Bill Trapp, the white man, is rejected as he painfully tries to return to life through his new Negro friends who live in Beetlecreek. Mr. Demby has informed me that the title of the novel ". . . came from an image in one of Thomas Wolfe's works, where a beetle was run over by a car and squashed on an overheated highway."

The narrowness and hypocrisy of the Negro community living in a mean little town which denies fulfillment to its own people is symbolically represented as a coffin. Thus, a character says, "You're the only one who ever knew what a coffin this town was." Again, Demby writes:

"It was a melancholy fall night and it made Johnny

very sad. And Black Enameled Death that he had seen represented everything of Beetlecreek . . ."

The heart of the book exists in the dynamic counterpoint of the relationship between Bill Trapp, the old white man, and his Negro friend, David. Both men live in a past of half-forgotten memories and hopes that have become vague longings. They are both lonely, and Demby writes that David ". . . could tell that the old man was lonely, and this moved him. This, at least, he could understand." Both the white man and the Negro are trapped in the town of Beetlecreek and both must withhold feeling because they have learned that in their world to express emotion is to invite danger. Demby writes: "Bill Trapp held tight inside himself and wouldn't let himself feel anything."

But this theme of repression has a special meaning in the life of the Negro man who is a talented artist. During his youth, Johnny's uncle, David, discovered the rich world of books and music, had hoped to become a person of culture and refinement, to find love and to realize his potential as an artist. But repeatedly in the novel, Demby tells the reader of how the world of Beetlecreek suffocates hope, and reduces life to insectile crawling.

David had:

". . . the feeling of being suffocated and unable to move. This had nothing to do with his not having opportunities or 'civil rights', but it was a strange feeling, very difficult for him to explain to himself, which had to do with feeling Death, feeling frozen, suffocated, unable to breathe, knowing there was little to be done about it. . . . And it wasn't long before he discovered what these other means of escape were, and he learned about goodtiming with girls and drinking. This was the easiest way, and you could goodtime yourself out of being suffocated. . . .

". . . suddenly he realized that he was getting used to the goodtiming. More and more difficult was it becoming to find the real secret of escape. And of this, he was afraid, but he had no strength to change. The easy way kept coming back to him with ever increasing strength until there was no more looking at pictures, no more reading books, no more listening to music, only the goodtimes and the easy way to escape the feeling of the death–grip."

In describing the crisis of David's life Demby deals with the forces of repression and inhibition among Negroes, and he effectively communicates the tragic implications of these processes which have perhaps a special meaning for Negro intellectuals.

Demby writes:

". . . as soon as he saw one person, as soon as he heard one person speak, the vision would disappear and being in the death–grip would seem the most natural and permanent thing in the world.

"Then he would go back to goodtiming, all the while feeling himself getting deeper and deeper and the death-grip becoming stronger and stronger. More and more he became a kind of clown and less and less he was a man, and more and more he was like the rest of them, and all together they goodtimed their way into forgetting the death–grip."

In the episode of the killing of the pigeon in the gang's shack in the book, little Johnny's natural impulse of protective tenderness for the frightened bird is thwarted and instead there is a senseless act of cruel violence. But Johnny's need to belong is finally so urgent that he relinquishes his instinctive feeling in order to be accepted by the group and to no longer be an outsider. His initiation into the only society offered him is a destructive act, and in exercising it he proves that he, too, can be cruel and violent. In an overpowering resolution of the novel's conflicts, Johnny commits the final act, expressing his anguish. At the end of the book his Uncle David tries one last time to "goodtime" his way out of Beetlecreek and the story is complete.

The powerless need a sense of community because that is all they can draw from. If not accepted there, then where will they be accepted? But Demby tells us that there is no salvation in being accepted even by your own community. No salvation in becoming a part of the group if that means a violation of the self. On either side of acceptance lies de-

189

struction, there is no salvation in alternatives. David leaves, Johnny joins. Both are trapped. There is only stagnation and suffocation for all the inhabitants of all the Beetlecreeks.

We all have our private fantasies. The whites need Negroes, the Negroes need whites, and we populate each other's dreams. As for the characters in *Beetlecreek*, love must be repressed, tender impulses transformed, desires feared, and there is no salvation.

The theme and material of *Beetlecreek* is the subject matter of great literature. There are limitations in the treatment of *Beetlecreek* which suggest that the novel might have been expanded to further realize the rich potential of its theme. This would have led to an even more fully developed novel. The material in the work of a great writer reverberates back through experience so that what is evoked in the reader is more than the dimensions of what is written. What one could call, I suppose, the novel's fourth dimension, the commentary that is always larger than that which is described.

William Demby in this book is possessed with a powerful idea, and he tells the story well. His limitation is that his ideas are not fully confronted. In *Beetlecreek* he just misses making the leap into that place where great writing lies. A judgment cannot stand on promise, but the talent and sensibility revealed in *Beetlecreek* suggests that in his future work Demby will make that leap. This limitation aside—bearing in mind that the novel is the work of a young writer and a first novel at that—*Beetlecreek* is not only memorable fiction, but a justifiable claim can also be made for it as a significant work in our literature. Demby has written a unique tale with courage and honesty, and the control that he exhibits must be considered remarkable in the work of a neophyte writer.

Beetlecreek represents a significant departure from the sociological tradition of the literature of American Negroes. In this work Demby has refused to be limited to the conventional Negro themes of the past. The author is not writing to amuse a white audience nor to propagandize for his fellow Negroes. He is transmuting into literature the materials of that part of the American experience which is *Beetlecreek*, an experience that is shared by both Negroes and whites.

Herbert Hill
New York, January 1967

From the AVON ◆ Library

Alfred Grossman

    ACROBAT ADMITS   VS13   75¢

John Barth

    THE FLOATING
      OPERA   VS5   75¢

    END OF THE ROAD   GS2   50¢

Irvin Faust

    ROAR LION ROAR   SS5   60¢

James Purdy

    MALCOLM   VS6   75¢

    THE NEPHEW   SS12   60¢

    COLOR OF DARKNESS
      and CHILDREN
      IS ALL   W108 $1.25